Easy as Pie

D1518680

CARINA TAYLOR

For the ones who see a hill and have zero urge to hike it.

Content Warning

Hi there readers! I'm a romcom writer. I write things to make you laugh, smile, snort, and all manner of good stuff.

But my characters still struggle with real things. Trauma, loss, anxiety, etc.

In Easy as Pie, there is the discussion about a main character losing her mother to cancer. This is a very heavy topic, so PLEASE, if this makes you uncomfortable, don't read.

Not all books are for all people, and I don't want to be the one to hurt you.

P.S. This is a closed-door romcom—all of the sizzle but no open-door scenes.

Chapter 1

Hazel

There are three unanswered texts on my phone.

Three notifications glaring at me in red. I can't stand having those there.

Do I open my phone and get rid of it?

Nope. I saw the preview of those texts, and like a complete idiot, I have my phone settings set to send read receipts. It's like I was born yesterday rather than twenty-six years ago.

If I open the texts...*he'll* know. And then I'll have to answer him.

I haven't answered his texts or phone calls since he moved back to town.

Like any true friend, I have continued to send him hilarious reels on social media. And because he's civilized, he doesn't call out my lack of text messaging in our DM's.

The previews of the text read:

"Hey! I'm back in tow—" I could only guess that he was

1

back in town. Being "back in towel" didn't make as much sense.

"**Dinner this week—**" He could have meant that he was eating dinner this week. But more likely he was wanting to get dinner together.

"**Hello. Earth to Hazel—**" Okay, so he might be on the verge of breaking friend protocol and *calling* me. But I'll worry about that later.

So, I keep that phone in the pocket of my sweatpants.

All I need is tampons. One simple yet crucial item. It's eight o'clock at night, and it's hopefully past the time that I'll see anyone I know in this Publix grocery store, which is good because I look like a bridge troll today.

Someday, I'll be brave enough to try period underwear, and I won't have to do these late-night shopping sprees.

When you're expecting D-day, it's okay to look like a troll. At least, that's what my mom always told me. I grew up thinking that you couldn't have your period unless you were wearing sweatpants, and I think she was the most wonderful mother for letting me believe that. There's not a day that I don't miss her.

I check both ways before I turn down the feminine hygiene aisle.

This town is big enough to avoid everyone you know if you're dressed for the Oscars but small enough to run into every person you've ever met while I am wearing my holey sweats and have a giant pimple on my chin.

Ohhhh, which reminds me, I need to buy a gallon of chocolate milk...all for myself. Because I live alone. I don't even have a cat, which might explain my life's current lonely state.

If I had a cat, I wouldn't feel the need for companionship.

I grab the product I need when I hear a voice that nearly drops me to my knees.

"Could I get a couple of filets of that salmon?"

Ew. Fish on ice. Nasty. But that's not what makes my heart skip a beat.

I would know that voice anywhere.

My heart lurches as I imagine running down the aisle and tackling the man belonging to that voice with a giant hug. Smothering him with the joy of seeing him...

But lucky for me, reason takes over.

I can*not* tackle my best friend, whom I secretly crushed on in college. I'm sure I'm totally over that, but it's been so long since I've seen him. I can't risk it tonight.

And I *cannot* face him looking like the death angel with bad acne. Especially when I haven't been answering his texts and avoiding him ever since he came home.

The meat counter is off the end of the tampon aisle. A tall man stands facing the butcher, his back to me. But I'd know that wavy brown hair anywhere. Granted, those shoulders have bulked up more than I remember, but I know that athletic build that's visible beneath the scrubs he's wearing.

Honestly, I don't know how I will face him again. The shock I felt when I realized my best friend was the most attractive man I'd ever met...I still haven't recovered. And I'm scared I'll *still* be attracted to him when I face him again.

When we met up over the summer during my senior year of college, we decided to go swimming.

Swimming = shirtless Tripp.

I drooled. I wish that drooling was a figurative description, but I'd drooled so hard that Tripp had been concerned I was choking on a chip.

It's a deep level of mortification that I'm not sure I'll ever recover from.

His low voice rumbles toward me again. "Oh, that one looks perfect."

I never knew I'd be jealous of a cold fish. I hug the box of tampons and slowly step backward.

Directly into the side display for another brand of feminine products.

The cardboard crashes down, and packages of pads land with rapid-fire splats.

Not good. Not good at all if I want to avoid being seen. Nothing is broken, so I don't stay to fess up to my crime.

Leaping over the boxes, I sprint to the end of the aisle and glance around. I spot an open checkout stand and head there with determination, skill, and grace.

Actually, none of those things.

I'm too busy looking over my shoulder to make sure Tripp Sharpe isn't lurking there, watching me epically embarrass myself.

Which is the only reason I can find for what happens next.

My left foot hits something hard and orange. I clutch the tampon box, but the cardboard flip rips open beneath my grip.

I trip over the decorative pumpkin sticking out from under the conveyor belt and launch forward. My elbows hit the conveyor belt, and the tampon box flies out of my hand, hitting the cashier in the face and shooting tampons all over the floor behind him.

The poor small child. Looks like he's fresh into college and maybe has his first job. And I just shot tampons at him.

"Ouch, dang it," I gripe when the conveyor belt pinches my arm fat.

That'll teach me to push up my sweater sleeves. There's nothing to protect my arm hairs from the rubber belt.

After a few unsuccessful attempts, I finally manage to stand upright, pull down my sweater sleeves and make a feeble effort to look the cashier in the eye.

"Er, sorry about that. There's a pumpkin right there, and I—" I cut myself off and lean forward to pull a tampon off his name tag. "Glen. So incredibly sorry. Let me just—"

He shakes his head and picks up the intercom phone. "Don't worry. I'll have someone bring you a new box."

And then, it's over the intercom before I can sneeze at him to stop. I rest both elbows on the counter and plant my face in my hand as I hear the loudspeaker through the store.

"Can someone bring a box of tampons, size regular, to register four?"

I'm going to die. Right here. Register 4. Puddle of embarrassment. It would be a straightforward mystery for someone to solve.

Hazel Preston shot tampons at a stranger and then had her embarrassment replayed over the loudspeaker. Of course, she's dead. Cause of death: mortifying embarrassment.

This is the kind of stuff that happened to me in high school. I somehow always landed myself in a scrape. This is *not* what happens to boring adult Hazel. Absolutely not.

Yet here I am, watching a very helpful someone with a name tag that says 'Debbie' hurry forward and hand another box to Glen.

"Thank you, Debbie," he says.

I offer her a very, very weak smile of thanks. That's all I've got. The last vestiges of a functioning human are given to Debbie. I hope I never see Glen or her ever again.

Unfortunately, while I'm at my most embarrassing level, I spot a familiar dark-brown head moving back and forth behind the bread display. Oh no. If Tripp walks past that bread display, he'll see me in all my sweatpants glory.

I pivot to face Glen like he's my favorite person in the whole wide world.

He rings up the box, and I practically throw cash at him. All I want to do is run out of this store and never have to set foot in here again. My ego couldn't handle it.

I'll drive to Ashville for my groceries from now on.

Besides, it'll be a lot easier to avoid my best friend if we don't shop at the same store anymore.

"Hazelnut?" a deep, shocked voice behind me asks.

Apparently, the bread display wasn't as amazing as I had hoped. Because my best friend, Tripp Sharpe, is standing directly behind me.

I slowly turn around to face him.

Easy smile showing straight white teeth. A little scruff that accentuates those strong cheekbones and jawline. Sparkling green eyes.

Nope. He's still as attractive as sin since the three years I last saw him.

"Tripp? I didn't see you."

"What are you doing here?" he asks excitedly with a big smile on his face.

"Oh, you know, just buying milk and eggs," I reply with a smile.

He stares at the box in my hand, but then his attention moves back up to the messy bun of hair on my head. "Oh, you've got a—little—"

He points at the hair, and I can tell he's fighting back laughter. My stomach flops as I think of all the possible things that could be there. None of them are great options.

"Hazel, you have a tampon stuck in your hair."

I blink twice, then clear my throat. "Oh yes, I've started keeping them there. That way I have it whenever I need it, you know. Don't want to be caught by surprise."

He steps forward, pulls the tampon from my hair and sets it on the conveyor belt. "There. All better."

Then he sets down his few groceries on the belt. I swallow the lump in my throat and am happy to realize I'm not drooling this time. When he turns around, he stretches his muscly arms wide, and I'm reminded of his wingspan right before he hugs me tight to his firm chest. Zit and all.

Chapter 2

Tripp

The pungent smell of kettle corn fills the air. Do people actually eat that stuff? As a child, I had one bite of it, expecting it to be caramel corn...I've never overcome that betrayal.

I try to push past the kettle corn smell, breathing deeply as I pass a cotton candy cart, hoping to erase that kettle corn stench.

A child's scream whips through the air. A ghost flies by, and a witch tips her hat to me.

Yup. I made it to the annual Harvest Hollow Fall Festival for the first time in almost ten years.

With so much time in between visits, I'd expected it to feel different.

But *nooooo.*

Same pie baking contest. Same 5k beer run. Same pumpkin carving contest. The atmosphere is the essence of a happy fall—the same as it was when I was a kid.

The festival used to only pull in people from

surrounding counties, but I had heard that in the last couple of years it has gained in popularity, and more of out-of-staters have shown up. Lucky for me, I still see a lot of familiar faces of Harvest Hollow residents working the booths. I even spot some kids I remember from middle school running around with their own kids in tow.

Someday, I hope that will be me. A mini-Tripp running with me through a festival. And a Mrs. Tripp I'm head over heels for. I've yet to meet someone I could care that deeply for, and so instead, I'm the single guy moving back home while kids I grew up with are already halfway to being grandparents by now.

It's good to be home. To see some familiar faces.

But there is one person in particular I'm determined to find.

Hazel. I haven't seen her since running into her at the grocery store. She had been so embarrassed about the tampons, and it didn't seem like a good night to try and reconnect.

When Hazel and I were eleven, we ended up on the wrong end of a dodgeball game together. She jumped in front of me to save me from a hit. The ball gave her a bloody nose that made her pass out. From that day on, we were best friends.

Hazel has stayed in Harvest Hollow all this time while I've been off attending school and doing residencies. I haven't seen her in over three years. I've been home to visit twice during that time, but life worked against us, and I wasn't able to spend time with her.

Hazel Preston is priority number one tonight. I *will* lay eyes on my best friend if it's the last thing I do. And I know she's here, because she would never miss a Harvest Festival.

"Dr. Tripp Sharpe!"

An *unfortunate* last name, but one that my surgeon father thinks is hilarious.

I spin at the sound of my name and come face to face with my sixth-grade teacher, Mrs. Perkins.

Not exactly who I was hoping to see, but she's a sweetheart, so I'll actually acknowledge that I heard my name.

"Mrs. Perkins," I greet her with a smile. Because you can't help but smile when she's grinning so brightly at you. She still has those gray curly bangs that were in style in the '80s and bright pink glasses. Her cheeks are rosy, and it's hard to tell if she just has a happy personality or if she's a closet alcoholic.

She's the only teacher who has bothered to keep up with me. I was a middle school smart aleck, and Mrs. Perkins was an optimistic saint.

It's been a while since I've been back, so I applied and landed a six-month job here. My work as a locum tenens physician—a.k.a. a traveling doctor—has given me a chance to move home, at least for a little while.

"Did your mom volunteer you at the beanbag toss booth?"

I smile to cover my grimace. My mom, the dentist—Dr. Celeste Sharpe. She never misses an opportunity to share her knowledge of good dental health, and she sets up a booth every year at the Harvest Festival to hand out toothbrushes and floss to kids.

Like a good son, I'd already visited her booth before I went in search of Hazel.

"Pretty sure she's making the kids floss before letting them play whatever game she has set up." I glance at a group walking by, my eyes landing on a blonde head. The woman turns to the side, and I see that it is *not* Hazel.

Mrs. Perkins—I'm sure she has a first name, but I've never heard it—pats my arm. "We all know and love your mother and we have healthy teeth, thanks to her. And now we won't have to worry about our health with you working in the emergency room."

Her optimism is not unfounded this time. I found my niche, and I do well in it. Emergencies? Yes. Love 'em. For some reason, I'm able to detach in an emergency. The emotion hits later after I have dealt with the problems.

I see someone else with blonde hair walk by in the crowd, and it catches my attention.

"I bet I know who you're looking for..." Mrs. Perkins teases as she follows my eyes this time.

I try to look as innocent as possible, but she winks. "She's at the tire tent with her dad. They're running some type of game that will probably land someone in your emergency room."

I straighten my shoulders and smile at the thought. The thought of seeing Hazel, that is, not of someone getting hurt. "Thank you, Mrs. Perkins. I haven't seen her in a while."

"She's such a good girl," she announces as she waves me off.

Good girl? What does that even mean? Who on earth would refer to Hazel as a "good girl?" My personal experience has been vastly different.

Street races organized in high school? Hazel.

Graffiti on the train? Hazel.

Defaming her sister's ex-boyfriend on the town water tower? Hazel.

I laugh as I walk away. Hazel is many things, but I'd never label her as "good."

Fun. Bright. Entertaining. Loyal. Best friend in the whole wide world. Now those are some titles that fit her better than "good."

I move through the crowd, looking for some activity that looks like it's Hazel-organized.

And then I see it. A tower of tires stacked on top of each other sitting next to a tent. A pumpkin rests on top, and a line of kids are launching balls at it.

Beside the wobbly tower of tires, I spot a pair of booted feet on a cooler and follow them to a pair of coveralls and a crop of messy blonde hair piled on a head. She's relaxing in a camp chair as if she doesn't have a care in the world.

A grin stretches across my face, and my heart starts beating loudly. Or maybe that's the band on stage a couple tents down. Either way, I'm ridiculously happy to lay eyes on that blonde head.

This is coming home. It's been way too long since I've seen my best friend. One quick grocery store run-in wasn't enough. That hug barely counted.

She has a sucker poking out of the side of her mouth, and she grins as a particularly enthusiastic kid chucks a softball at the pumpkin. It hits, but the pumpkin stays where it sits.

The relaxed figure in the chair pulls the red lollipop out of her mouth to say, "Chase, try the bowling ball."

The lollipop disappears back into her mouth as the kid, Chase, grins at her. He bends down to retrieve a bowling ball. Unfortunately, behind that tall tower of tires is a pie tent. A bowling ball getting lobbed through the air probably isn't in line with the festival's safety regulations.

"Hazel Preston, are you being a bad influence?"

Wide, innocent blue eyes turn to stare at me in surprise. She removes the lollipop from her mouth with a loud pop, then grins at me. Her lips are stained red from the cherry, and her teeth aren't much better.

Mom would be horrified.

She waves the lollipop through the air like a scepter. "Hold that thought on the bowling ball, Chase. The fun police have arrived."

Chase's shoulders sag in disappointment, and I march over to stand next to her camp chair. "Fun police, hey?"

She shrugs and looks up at me with feigned innocence. My breath catches when I stare at her. Have I ever noticed that Hazel is beautiful? I'm sure I have. I take a deep breath when I realize my heart's beating fast. No, this is not going to happen. I absolutely cannot find my Hazel attractive. It's desperation sneaking out. I'm sure of it.

I shrug off the notion and hold a hand out to her, but when she grasps it, she jerks hers back quickly.

I look at her, wondering if she *has* outgrown our friendship, and I don't like the panic that wells up in my chest. But then she says, "Oops. Static electricity." She stands up on her own and smiles as she throws her arms toward me.

She's happy to see me. As I open my arms, my grin is so big it's hurting my face. She wraps me up in a giant bear hug, just about squeezing the life out of me.

I return the favor.

"It's been way too long." I lift her off the ground. I would be tempted to spin around in a circle if I didn't know she got dizzy.

Three years have gone by since we hung out. It doesn't matter if I think she's changed, or that I'm now noticing that she's a woman and we're not kids anymore.

Three years is way too long to go without seeing your best friend. Especially if it's making me notice things about her that I shouldn't be noticing.

"You never came to visit me," I snap as she pulls out of my arms.

She plants her hands on her hips and glares up at me. "It's a two-way airport."

I shrug. "Touché."

"Why *didn't* you ever come to visit me?" I ask as we walk past the bumper car station, where happy shrieks fill the air. It's unfair of me to ask that, since the last time I'd texted and invited Hazel to come visit, her dad had fallen and knocked his hip out.

"Why didn't *you* come to visit me?" she fires back.

Shrugging, I say, "I guess we're going to keep going back and forth on this. My best excuse is medical school and residencies kept me busy."

She smiles and points at my chest with a slender finger with a painted-orange nail. "I'm glad to see you don't wear your doctor's coat everywhere."

"I try to blend in with the plebeians at least occasionally. I want to know if I can still relate to people like you." I give an extra drag on the "u."

She leans forward and shoves my shoulder good-naturedly. "Come on, Your Highness. You can use the other camp chair while the kids try to knock the pumpkin off the top of the tire stack."

"I had something else in mind." I stare at her and raise my eyebrows.

She raises hers back. She whispers, "What did you have in mind?"

"Something fun," I whisper back.

"I'm in."

I hold out my hand to shake hers. "It's a deal. Let's go find your replacement."

Chapter 3

Hazel

This wasn't how I wanted to reconnect with Tripp again.

My best friend.

First, he sees me in the store with a tampon stuck in my hair, and now he catches me being a bad influence on middle school kids. Yeah, not my most shining moment. Also, not my *worst* moment, but I digress.

"Don't throw the bowling ball while we're gone," he says to Chase with an easy smile. Though Chase looks dejected, he nods in agreement and sets the bowling ball down.

Tripp flings an arm around my shoulders and directs me inside the open wall tent where Dad sits, sipping black coffee. I'm pretty sure he would bleed black coffee if he were to get cut.

"Biff! How are you?" Tripp releases his hold on my shoulders to go forward and shake Dad's hand. Dad has always liked Tripp. *Who hasn't?*

He's friendly to everyone he meets, never makes anyone

uncomfortable, and is happy to do a million favors for you even if he gets nothing out of the deal. I was the screwup in school, and he would patch up my mistakes—the perfect friendship.

Dad leverages himself out of the camp chair, hot coffee sloshing over the side of his mug and dripping onto his already-stained jeans.

"Good to see you, son!" He shakes Tripp's hand and then gives him one of those back slaps that rattle your teeth. "How have you been? You home now?"

"Yes, I work at Mercy General Hospital in the ER." He looks happy as he says it. I'm not surprised. He loves this little town and always has. "I've been back for two weeks now."

He side-eyes me at that, and I do my best to look innocent, even though I've been avoiding him since he moved home. The unfortunate attraction I discovered during our senior year of college has not dwindled with time. Avoiding Tripp has been my desperate attempt to maintain my friendship with him. It's a lot easier to stay friends over texting.

Thank goodness we didn't go to college together. Since high school, we've only seen each other on school breaks, but we've managed to rock this long-distance friendship thing.

"Good for you," says Dad. "I know Hazel will be happy to have you home; she doesn't have many friends here."

Could a sinkhole magically appear in the gravel? Because I'd happily jump into it right now.

Tripp bumps my arm with his. "Hazel's just selective. She only hangs out with the best of the best."

"When she's not training Milo, our new part-time

employee, she's working with me all day," Dad reminds him. It's not entirely accurate. Dad's been recovering from hip surgery and taking it easy as per the doctor's orders. He's busy with physical therapy appointments and doing the necessary exercises and icing to help it heal. I honestly can't wait to get back to working with him in the shop. I miss him.

"Exactly." Tripp winks. "The best."

Dad laughs.

I nudge Tripp's arm. "If you two are done making fun of me, I better make sure no kids are about to throw a bowling ball through the air."

"Hold up." Tripp taps my shoulder as I start to walk away. He turns back to my dad. "Do you mind if I steal Hazel for a while?"

Dad waves a hand toward the festival. "Go for it! I can keep these kids in line and hand out candy. Milo's here somewhere, he can help me." He turns around and grabs a bucket of candy. "I've got this under control."

Somehow, I'm pretty sure my dad doesn't have it under control. He's going to give kids way too much candy, someone will probably get hit in the head with a baseball, and they'll all have a blast in the meantime.

"Thanks, Dad!" Tripp leads the way out of the tent, pulling me along with him. His hand holds mine in a firm grip. He has a lot of callouses for a doctor, which come from his increasing love of the outdoors. I know he's spent the last couple years taking up hiking, kayaking, rafting, etc. Any outdoor activity he could get into, and it looks good on him. He seems more vibrant and energetic. Granted, medical school can suck the life out of anyone.

I ask, "What's first? Would you like to make the tour and visit with everyone you know?"

He groans. "Please, no."

Tripp's best-kept secret is that despite being fantastic with people, deep down, he's a raging introvert. I'm ninety percent sure that's why he chose to pursue being an emergency room doctor. There's not much time for small talk in those kinds of situations.

"Peggy wants me to visit the quilting tent." He clasps my arms. "Save me."

Peggy Grady is a Harvest Hollow lifer who breathes town gossip. If I can avoid her—I do.

"How do you feel about an overpriced corn dog and puking your guts up on a fair ride?"

"Yes to the first, no to the second."

"So, I'll have to settle for the Ferris wheel?"

"Sounds amazing." He grins, those familiar dimples popping out and doing something dangerous to me.

Those damn dimples are the reason I've tried to hide from Tripp ever since he moved back two weeks ago.

"I can't believe it's taken this long to hang out. I kept missing you when I stopped by your house last week." He looks at me and smiles again, utterly oblivious that at least one of those times, I was hiding in the back of the shop.

"It's really good to see you again, Tripp. I wasn't sure you'd ever come back." Well, now I sound like the whiny best friend that's never grown up. And while I *am* the whiny best friend, I have done some growing up. I've had to.

I just wish there was a way to rein in my feelings. I wish he'd visited more—but I also *need* to avoid him because Tripp is still very much Tripp, and as attractive as ever.

Basically, I'm in deep trouble because I don't know how to solve this pesky little problem.

"It's a shame you couldn't come see me this last year in Oregon. I think you would have liked it. But I always forget that you're not much of a traveler."

"Yup. That's right." It's what I want everyone to believe. It's what I desperately want to believe myself. But the lie is getting harder to swallow. Harder to hold in the reason that I never leave Harvest Hollow. Time to move onto safer conversation territory, so I ask, "How are your parents?"

"They're good. Mom's busy at her practice. Dad's well, still Dad and obsessing over work and golf."

"Your mom keeps telling me I need to come in for a visit."

We laugh at that. Tripp's dad is a surgeon, while his mom is the local dentist. It's a whole family of doctors. Tripp's dad isn't big on family bonding, or love, or anything outside of Tripp's achievements and scholastic abilities. My dad has been far more supportive of Tripp than his own father has, for as long as I've known him.

"Oh, look! There's the corn dog stand." Tripp reaches into his back pocket and pulls out his wallet while I pull out a few bills of cash.

He side-eyes me. I pretend not to notice while I walk a little faster, shifting closer to him.

My arm brushes against his as I crowd his space. His feet start to match my speed.

I take a deep breath, then stick out my foot, tripping and pushing him behind me as I hurry up to the trailer, slapping the bills on the counter as I gasp out, "Three corn dogs, please."

Tripp tries to reach around me to put his cash on the counter, but I stick my elbows out like I'm about to start the chicken dance.

The kid behind the counter stares at us as though he's never seen anyone fight over paying the bill. Maybe he hasn't. But it's good to win this round.

Ever since Tripp and I got our first jobs in high school, we've competed to pay the bill when we're out together. It's become an intense friendly competition that we both thrive on.

"Erm, no," I manage to squeak out. "Definitely my turn."

"You shouldn't have." *Why does his voice make it sound like a threat?*

"But I did," I tell him as he squeezes my arm. Goose-bumps travel up my arm, and not from the cold.

He chuckles at that, and I can feel my grin starting to hurt my cheeks. Now everything feels normal again. It's going to be okay. I can be best friends with him as though nothing has changed.

At least, I think I can...

Chapter 4

Tripp

Hazel's elbows are still weapons of mass destruction.

I'm slightly winded from the scuffle leading up to the corn dog trailer, and I just might have a bruise on my ribs tomorrow. But boy, did it feel good to see her lighten up again.

She had me worried for a minute.

She'd seemed tense since she laid eyes on me this evening. I can't say I blame her. She was probably wondering what our friendship would be like after all these years.

For me, it hasn't changed. I'm glad we can get past the initial awkward reunion and move forward to enjoying being around each other again. There's nothing better than an easy friendship.

And now I owe her for our next outing. After that scuffle, I'll make sure it's equally embarrassing.

Hazel spins around to pass me two steaming hot corn

dogs. "Here you go. If this doesn't land you in your own ER, I don't know what will."

"It's a risk I'm willing to take."

"I heard they were short-staffed there," she pries as she grabs a few ketchup packets and drops them into the pocket of her coveralls.

"They're hiring a couple of full-time positions, so hopefully that unfortunately true rumor is short-lived."

Hazel nods as she blows on the corn dog in her hand. "Want to do any rides for old times' sake?"

I smirk as I remember our senior year of high school and the not-buckled-roller-coaster seat. It involved me hanging on to Hazel so she wouldn't fall off. It still gives me the occasional nightmare. "Ferris wheel while we eat the corn dogs." I gesture to the lit-up Ferris wheel before taking a steaming hot bite. "Ow, ow, ow!"

Hazel reaches over and takes away both corn dogs with a scowl. "You still haven't learned not to bite into hot food? How did you survive all these years?"

"Through no fault of my own."

The teasing light leaves her eyes, and she shrugs. "You probably had lots of people taking care of you."

I think about my first stint as an ER resident doctor in Oregon.

My first real job after residency was in Oregon. I'd applied because I'd always wanted to experience the Pacific Northwest.

Getting that job was a dream come true. And the people I met there were amazing: my good friend Archie and his wife Meyer...Meyer's mom, who always had me over for dinner; Margaret, the town's honorary grandma, who welcomed me as if I was another of her town grandkids.

Archie Dunmore had been instrumental in my falling in love with the West Coast, and his in-laws had been incredibly welcoming to me while I lived there. I would love to take Hazel back with me next time I go.

"Yeah, you could say I've been taken care of. Now give those back to me." I reach for the corn dogs.

She rolls her eyes and hands them back to me. "I tried to warn you."

This time, I blow on it briefly before I take a big bite. Tastes like high school.

Hazel leads the way to the Ferris wheel, leans over, and pulls a string of tickets from one of her forty million pockets.

"Aren't you overheated in those things?" I ask. It's not hot outside, but walking around, eating hot food, and just the general heat from the cooking and all the people make it feel pretty warm. I'm glad I left my coat in my car.

"I was actually thinking I should have grabbed a bigger sweatshirt that I could wear over the coveralls. This corn dog is warming me up finally." She pulls a ketchup packet out of her pocket and passes it to me. I tear it open with my teeth and squeeze some onto hers and then mine. "Dad thought it would be good for business to wear the new coveralls with Biff's Towing and Tires written on the back."

"You're the picture-perfect walking advertisement." No one should look good in coveralls, but somehow Hazel does. Her petite stature and pile of blonde hair. Those red lips—still courtesy of the lollipop—make you think she's dressed up for a modeling gig. But underneath those coveralls I know there's a strong, capable body. She's a mechanic whiz with a sharp mind. She's the kind of best friend that challenges me to be a better version of myself.

She gives me a mock curtsy. "Why thank you, good sir."

We eat in silence as the line slowly moves forward.

I wonder if anyone has knocked the pumpkins off of the tire stack yet, or if any of the kids will be going to the ER tonight.

When it's our turn to get on the Ferris wheel, Hazel hands over the tickets, and we both climb on. It rocks precariously, and she points to the opposite side of the bucket with her corn dog stick. We sit down, facing each other.

"Can't be too careful," Hazel says with a smile as the Ferris wheel lurches into motion. "You know Ferris wheels are held together with one bolt, right?"

I glare at her as the Ferris wheel jerks and creaks as it picks up speed. I thought this would be a nice calm option. I was wrong. Anything with Hazel is lively. I still remember the death grip I had on Hazel when her buckle broke on that roller coaster. "I kind of hate you right now."

Hazel waits until we're halfway up the wheel to say, "Yup. One person forgetting to check the nut, and we're toast."

I point at her with the corn dog stick. "Stop."

"We could fall straight to that asphalt, right down there," she says as she freakin' stands up and leans over the side.

The bucket rocks, and I drop the corn dog stick, diving forward to grab the back of her coveralls and pull her back into her seat.

Now I'm kneeling on the gross sticky floor directly in front of her.

"What the—Hazel! Don't scare me like that!"

She shrugs nonchalantly, but her cheeks are turning

bright red, and her eyes flash as she asks me, "Why didn't you tell me you were still scared of heights? You texted me and told me you've been hiking every mountain you can find!"

I plant my hands on the bench on either side of her, almost ready to stand up, but the bucket wobbles again. "I did tell you that. But I'm hiking the mountain on my own two feet. I still have nightmares about that roller coaster ride."

She stops smiling. "I'm sorry; I won't try and tease you anymore. I thought you had gotten over it." She pats my hand like I'm a frail little thing that needs her reassurance. *She* was the one who almost died on that roller coaster and I'm the one being left nervous. Shouldn't she have some trauma from it?

"DID SHE SAY YES?" someone shouts at us from above.

I look up to see a woman's face dangling over the side of the bucket above us. She has a pair of glasses dangling precariously from a lanyard.

Hazel tips her head back to look up, then we both look at each other and bust up laughing. I'm kneeling down in front of her on one knee on a Ferris wheel. Of course, it seems like I'm proposing.

I tip my head back and yell back, "She hasn't decided yet!"

We start to crest the top of the Ferris wheel, and at that moment, our bucket and the other woman's bucket are parallel; she yells, "Maybe you should kiss him!"

Hazel's cheeks turn bright red as she looks anywhere but my face. I push up off the ground and sit on my bench, grinning at her.

"Aw, come on. Embarrassed to think about kissing me?"

She just looks at me and laughs. "You do realize somehow someone we know is going to hear about this?"

"Nah, we're safe. There are lots of out-of-towners here. I think talking about kissing is embarrassing you." Her cheeks look like they're about to burst into flames.

The Ferris wheel screeches to a halt when we reach the bottom. We disembark and I follow after Hazel, who's doing her best to get away.

"Wow, I don't know mentioning kissing could scare you away so fast," I call after her.

Hazel pivots and hurries back to me, reaching up and grasping my shoulders with her strong hands.

She plants a kiss on my cheek, and on instinct I reach an arm around to embrace her.

She tips her head back. "Quit challenging me, Sharpe."

My breath catches as I look into those eyes.

As we pull apart, we hear someone call *both* of our names.

As luck would have it, Mrs. Perkins was with the other woman who had been yelling at us from her bucket. Hazel's eyes widen as she glances at them over my shoulder. Both of them are heading our way and Hazel doesn't look too happy about it. "Dang it. She gossips."

"Well, then, let's give them something to talk about."

Hazel grins up at me and I swoop her into my arms, bending her over backwards. I don't put my lips on her face, because there are alarm bells ringing that I won't be able to stop with a cheek kiss. But with my back to Mrs. Perkins, she'll assume that I'm kissing Hazel for all I'm worth.

Hazel's shaking with laughter in my arms, also a good

mood killer when you're having weird thoughts about kissing your friend.

"Did she say yes?" Mrs. Perkins asks as she stops next to us, slightly out of breath. Her friend looks equally engrossed.

Hazel spins around to glare at her. "Annie. Good grief. He wasn't proposing."

Annie? She did have a first name! Was Hazel on a first-name basis with Mrs. Perkins?

Mrs. Perkins—she'll never be Annie to me—shrugs. "I figured it was only a matter of time before you two kids got married. I guess I was wrong. Have a great evening! Margie's already leaving me behind." She hurries to catch up with the woman who had been yelling at us on the Ferris wheel.

Hazel presses her lips together and narrows her eyes at me. "Look what you've done."

"Annie? How do you know Annie?" I demand. "Isn't she *Mrs.* Perkins?"

"Her husband passed away twenty years ago. She's dating Henry now," Hazel says, as though I should know who that is.

"Of course, I should have known," I reply dryly, the minute I remember Henry is one of three retired mechanics Hazel meets with regularly for coffee. I've met the mechanics, but I hadn't realized she still kept up with them. She spent a lot of time with them during her college years and they helped teach her all sorts of car-related things.

Hazel nudges my arm with her shoulder. "Are you jealous?"

"She was my Mrs. Perkins first," I grumble.

Hazel is two years younger than me, but because of her

summer birthday, she was only a year behind me in school. Still, I was the one who had *Annie* Perkins first.

"It's true." Hazel shrugs. "She talked about you, though, and I think her love for you helped me get a B in her writing class."

"Are you accusing Mrs. Perkins of having favorites?" I bump her arm with mine to return the favor and feel a little bad when it knocks her off balance.

I latch on to her shoulders and steady her. But then I find that my eyes keep going to her lips. The very ones that kissed my cheek moments ago.

"I'm not accusing Annie of anything. I'm just stating facts. You're a rule-follower, and people love you."

Hazel's smiling up at me as if her words don't cut me to the quick.

Chronic people pleasing. It's something I've struggled with and wrestled with, all of my life.

Thinking that my self-worth came from how well I could perform.

Hazel knows this, and I'm pretty sure it's why she dragged me into all sorts of misadventures. Forcing me to get rid of that stiff mask I wore everywhere. Which I'm trying to let go of now as an adult.

And what better way to do it than hanging with my best friend—the ultimate trouble-causer?

Chapter 5

Hazel

I'm in deep trouble.

When I heard that woman on the Ferris wheel last night yelling at us, I flashed back to a different time. A *fictional* time when Tripp didn't view me as a best friend, and would someday like to kneel in front of me for real.

And then he had to challenge me about the kiss. Tripp and I have always been comfortable with physical affection —big hugs, bumping elbows, practically wrestling to pay bills. But something felt different last night. And I wonder if Tripp felt it too.

I quickly squash that ridiculous idea because that's what it is. Ridiculous. Fantasies are not real, and imagining things like that doesn't make them come true.

It's okay. *We're* okay. I will *make* us okay. Tripp is someone I need.

This stupid attraction to my best friend will have to take a hike. I won't let it ruin my life—or my friendship with him. Especially if I have plans for my life. Plans I'm not completely sure how to execute, so I guess they're only half-plans. But those half-plans are the reminder I need that now is not the time to complicate things with strange feelings toward my best friend.

With that in mind, I fling open the door to the Cataloochee Mountain Coffee Shop. The walls are brick, but the dark color is offset by the big windows lining the front of the shop.

A wave of fresh ground coffee beans hits me like a happy hug.

I can practically taste the air. I march up to the counter. An "I Love You a Latte" chalkboard sign sits on the counter next to the register. Coffee culture-meets-dad-joke.

Heather, the shop manager, greets me with a smile. "Your usual?"

"Yes, thank you. You're the best."

It's not too busy yet, because I'm meeting some friends at six thirty in the morning.

Three gentlemen in their seventies and eighties. We sit at the Cataloochee Coffee Shop, sipping our morning mochas and talking about cars. It's the closest thing to a steady relationship I've had in a long time.

I go on lots of dates, but nothing seems to develop into more. Hanson is my most recent attempt at dating, and I like the guy. But we're both so busy with our businesses that we keep cancelling on each other. Maybe it's not meant to be.

I rest my purse on the counter and dig out some cash to throw in the tip jar, then wait as Samantha finishes adding a pile of caramel on top of the whipped cream. Bless her heart. I must look as tired as I feel.

She slides the cup to me. "You're an angel, as usual," I tell her.

She laughs and waves me off. I turn around and slowly walk to the table, careful not to slosh the coffee out of the mug.

"You're late," Floyd snaps out, his frown bunching his white eyebrows together. Mr. Precise is something I call him in my head. He's a problem-solver and advice-giver, and generally has high expectations that you'd better not disappoint.

"You're grumpy," I say, as I slide into the seat next to Jean.

"Good morning," Jean greets me. He's a dead ringer for Morgan Freeman, just add in a hint of a French accent. I could happily listen to him tell stories all morning long. Not to mention, he's the most stable of the group.

"Annie said Tripp proposed."

I slowly turn to stare down Henry, the fourth member of our little group, and also Annie Perkins's boyfriend.

"Tripp did not propose. He thought I was going to fall off the Ferris wheel and was trying to save me."

Jean pipes up, "I actually read about it on the Harvest Hollow Happenings page."

That stinkin' anonymous Instagram account. It's the gossip rag of Harvest Hollow. No one knows who runs it, but whoever it is seems to know a lot about the born-and-raised Harvest Hollow crowd.

"The page was wrong, Jean."

Floyd's sharp eyes watch me over the top of his tea. "You sure? A man doesn't get on his knee for just anyone."

"Did y'all get together and discuss the rumored proposal this morning?" I say it jokingly, but then they all nod.

"Good grief. You can't even trust your friends to not talk behind your back anymore."

"We never said you should trust us," Floyd points out very helpfully.

Jean twists his latte around and then says, "But we do wonder if you'll be with us long."

"I'm not dying!"

"We mean marriage." Henry drags out the M word. Despite having a prolific dating life, he has strong sentiments about marriage—and they're not happy ones.

"Tripp is my best friend." I hold up my hands as if that explains everything, and I stand up. "There's no attraction there."

Three hums meet my ears.

"That's it. I'm not even going to tell you about the Ford GT that I have in the shop right now."

Jean pats my hand. "We're just teasing. Sit down and tell us about it."

They all share a secret look that I can't decipher.

"But," Henry says, "maybe you should think about getting a boyfriend. That way, people don't make the same mistake we just did."

Get a boyfriend. As easy as that. I try not to laugh. It's not like I have a problem meeting people...it's that I have a problem trying to run my business, run my dad's business, take online classes, and be a mediocre assistant helping to plan the Harvest Hollow Cancer Research Benefit dinner.

A boyfriend would be great, if I could find a low-maintenance one who will understand if I have to choose replacing brake pads over dinner with him.

I decide to ignore that lovely piece of Henry-style advice and hopefully get some good advice about a car.

My three mentors had all been acquaintances of my dad. When they found out that his daughter had an interest in becoming a mechanic, they essentially adopted me, teaching me tips and tricks you can only learn from years of work.

If it weren't for them, I wouldn't be able to do half the things I do.

Granted, I was on my own learn how to fix electric boards and working on electric cars is a completely different ballpark. Still, it's great to have a group of knowledgeable mechanics to turn to when I'm stumped.

And that stinkin' drive shaft. Those broken bolts are more important than my lack of a love life.

Chapter 6

Hazel

After coffee with the guys, I go back to the shop. I still live on my dad's property, in a small apartment above the large shop where I do my mechanic work. Dad still lives in the house I grew up in. When Mom was alive, she kept it decorated in full fall style around this time of year. Kara, my sister, kept up the tradition as a way to honor mom's memory.

This is our first fall since Kara moved away. She was so much like Mom that she kept us going with traditions, and dinners, and making Dad and me do some socializing. It wasn't a fair burden to her, and I'm glad she's moved on and getting a fresh start.

But now that it's just Dad and me living on the property, we're well on our way to becoming hermits.

Avoiding people has started to become our MO.

I think that's why I hadn't realized how good it would be to see Tripp—until he was standing in front of me (the second time; I refuse to think about the tampon incident).

I've done everything I can to avoid him these last few years. And when I heard he was moving home to Harvest Hollow, I went into full-on stealth mode to hide from him.

The number of imaginary transmissions I've replaced...sheesh.

I thought it would be better to stay away from him...but last night at the Harvest Festival, I realized how much I need our friendship. Maybe I can push past this attraction.

I *will* be Johnny Cash and walk this line. I'll be careful not to spend too much time with him, at least until I get a boyfriend or something. Henry's suggestion taking root...

I need something to distract me from this unfortunate attraction.

Hmmm. Maybe it's time to keep that date with Hanson. I've been a little busy with the shop and running the towing side of the business since Dad had his hip replacement.

My phone rings with the work ringtone. I've funneled all calls to my personal cell since Dad's still recovering. I don't trust him not to sneak around and try to work, and cause some permanent damage to his hip again.

"Hi there, I found your phone number when I searched for towing companies near Harvest Hollow, North Carolina. Did I reach the right place?"

"You did. What can I do for you?" I ask.

"Well, my car isn't running anymore." He chuckles. He doesn't sound like he's from around here.

Customers with a sense of humor, I'll take them any day. "That does sound like a problem. Can you tell me where you are?"

"I don't suppose telling you I'm parked next to a big oak tree would mean anything?"

"No, it would not."

"Dang. I'd heard Harvest Hollow was a small town. I've been dying to say, 'down by the oak tree.'"

"Hey now, we're not quite that small. And we have *three* oak trees." *More like three thousand.*

"Now I know you're teasing me. Can I text you my pinned location for the tow truck driver?"

"That, I can definitely work with."

He hangs up, and in a few short seconds, I have a location about a mile and a half outside town. I wash the grease off my hands in the shop sink, using the pumice soap to cut it. Then I head out of the shop and follow the driveway that leads over to Dad's house.

We're right on the edge of town on a two-acre lot. It's a perfect location for pulling in the big tow truck and having room to work on cars.

I run up the steps, swing the front door open and poke my head inside the house. I know Dad will be in the living room resting from his surgery. He'd better be doing his exercises like that doctor told him, or else we're going to have some words. "Dad, I got a call for a broken-down car outside town. I'll be back in about thirty."

He peers at me over the notebook he's writing in while he sits in his recliner. "Okay! I'll be here making phone calls for the benefit dinner. My favorite part."

His face looks as though he'd rather be doing anything but making phone calls, so I hurry out of there before he can talk me into taking on that task.

I fire up the tow truck and can't help but smile as I listen to the motor purr.

Our new tow truck is so much quieter and smoother than the old beater we've had since I was a child.

Old beaters might build memories, but they also blow eardrums.

The truck has to warm up a few minutes before I can take off, and I spend some time scrolling social media and doing a little light stalking of Tripp's pages.

I've seen all these pictures before, but I'm just giving myself a refresher course before I see him again.

His most recent pictures are of various lakes and mountains in Oregon. There's a picture of him and a dark-haired man standing together next to a set of kayaks. That must be the friend in Oregon he texted me about.

There's a picture of a birthday cake—it looks homemade, as though someone treated him special on his birthday. And I wasn't there.

When the truck's ready, I set the phone down and pull out of the driveway. I'll have to go straight through town to pick up the caller. Luckily, this thing runs quietly and smoothly even when I hit that unavoidable pothole at the intersection of Maple and Vine.

Downtown doesn't look too busy this morning. Everyone's probably sleeping off their busy festival weekend. The Cataloochee Mountain Coffee Shop is the busiest place at nine in the morning.

When I spot a car stranded on the side of the road just out of town, I figure this is my guy. I park the tow truck on the side of the shoulder directly in front of the car and read the text from Tripp.

Tripp: you haven't been avoiding me on purpose, have you?

Yes, I have Tripp, ol' boy.

Hazel: LOL, don't be ridiculous.

Even if you're right.

Tripp: It's just felt like we haven't been able to connect, and hanging out this weekend was great.

Hazel: I agree! Work's just been busy, and I wanted to give you time to spend with your family.

Also, not completely true. Unless Tripp's dad has undergone a steep personality change, then he and Tripp don't get along.

Tripp: So, we're good?

Hazel: 1000%.

I can't wait on his response, so I slip my phone into my pocket and climb out of the truck. I have a stranded out-of-towner to save.

A sedan with steam leaking out of the hood is parked barely off the road. Good thing this is on the straight stretch where people have time to scoot over.

The man sitting in the car climbs out. He's youngish. Somewhere around my age. Mid to late twenties. Good-looking, but not in the same way as Tripp, who makes you look twice or blush when he smiles at you.

I press my lips together, disappointed in how often my thoughts drift back to Tripp—*my very platonic best friend.*

"You must be who I talked with on the phone," the man says by way of greeting. "Thanks for getting out here so fast."

"Of course. What seems to be the problem?"

He points at the car where the hood is steaming. "A smoking problem. I keep telling him he needs to quit."

I smile at that. It's something Tripp would say. *And that*

will be the last time you compare this poor, unsuspecting stranger to Tripp.

Repeat after me, Hazel: Tripp is my best friend, and I will not find him ridiculously attractive. "Do you want me to look at it here or at the shop?"

"What would be the difference?"

"A towing fee," I say as I point to the hood. "If you pop that open, I'll see if it can get fixed here."

He smiles back. "Okay, then here would be great."

He climbs into the driver's seat and pops the hood. I slip my hand underneath, feeling for the latch. I find it, lift the hood the rest of the way, and prop it open. After taking a cursory look, it seems to be an easy fix. "Have you been driving a long way?"

"Does Reno count?"

I nod, using the long sleeve of my sweater to loosen the radiator cap. It'd burn me if I grabbed it with my bare hands. My love of cozy sweaters pays off with my job.

"I think you have an easy fix here. We'll see."

Fifteen minutes later, he starts it up again after the car has completely cooled and I've added more coolant.

No smoke.

No steam.

Just a regular running engine.

"Is now a good time to say I don't know much about cars?" he asks sheepishly.

Because he's been so nice, I refuse to make him feel bad for it. "Overheating is very common on long drives. If your car is constantly running at top temperature, it burns through the fluid a lot faster. Maybe just check in on it a little more often."

"Unfortunately, I'm that guy that takes his car to the shop for oil changes and any other refills," he says with a shrug.

I showed him the bottle I used. "Just look for the coolant. You'll do fine. Almost every gas station will have this there."

"Thanks, but I don't have any more long drives planned. Harvest Hollow is my destination. I can't believe I made it this far only to break down beside the oak tree." He tips his head toward the tree.

This time, I laugh and point at the "oak" tree. "That's a maple."

He mutters a good-natured curse. "Am I at least close to The Maple Tree Inn and Suites? That's my destination."

"It's right at the edge of town, so you're close," I reply before I turn to head back to the tow truck.

"Wait! How do I pay my bill?"

I point to the name on the side of the truck. Biff's Towing and Tires.

He looks at me with one raised eyebrow. "Don't tell me you're Biff."

"Nah, I run the shop out back. Hazel's Hot Wheels." Hazel's Hot Wheels was the name of my shop when I was twelve. Tripp and I came up with it. I still haven't come up with a real name. People bring their cars for me to fix—so I do.

The man laughs, "Well it's great to meet you, Hazel. I'm Adam Reeves. Maybe we'll see each other again."

I smile and wave as I climb in and fire up the truck.

What a *nice* man. Pleasant. Funny. Not Tripp. Can't even remember his name, even though I'm pretty sure he just said it. How unfortunate.

Maybe he'll have more car trouble in the future. He

could be the perfect distraction from all things Tripp-related. Henry would be so proud of me for thinking like this.

And I could use a distraction.

Because there's a text on my phone waiting for me.

Tripp: I'm going to be hungry after my 24-hour shift. I get off at 7. Want to grab dinner?

Hazel: Wish I could, but I'm replacing a transmission.

Do I usually replace transmissions at dinnertime? I do now.

Chapter 7

Tripp

S eeing Hazel this weekend felt like coming home. Trying to find her was like playing a live-action game of whack-a-mole.

But now that we've reconnected, it will be like it was growing up.

I have to get this weird attraction under control, because there was an odd minute there when I was kneeling in front of her on the Ferris wheel...where I wondered what it would be like if I *had* been proposing to Hazel.

It's a preposterous idea, and I have no clue why it jumped into my head. Which is why I have to stop thinking about it.

I still can't believe it took so long to hang out with her. My schedule's been busy, but not *that* busy.

Granted, she said she's busy, but that's not surprising.

What's surprising is that she hasn't texted me or tried to hang out *after* work—even after I'd told her I was home.

The Hazel I know is the queen of late nights and very little sleep.

She keeps saying she's replacing transmissions. And I might not be an expert on engines, but even *I* know there's more to it than that. There can't be that many broken-down transmissions in the world, not in a town the size of Harvest Hollow.

Besides, it's not like Hazel is the only mechanic in town. People could hypothetically take their cars somewhere else if she's slammed.

Which leaves the possibility that she's intentionally avoiding me. I've been worried that maybe she's outgrown our friendship, but then the way we eased back into it at the festival felt so natural.

Honestly, it was a relief.

I'd started to panic at the thought of not having Hazel as a best friend. What would I do without Hazel in my life?

Sure, I've got Archie now; I consider him a good friend. Maybe even best friend number 2. But he's not Hazel.

I press my fist against my forehead, trying to clear my thoughts and the lurking headache trying to force itself front and center.

When I took the position at the Mercy General Hospital ER, I was under the impression I would work four twelves. Instead, they snuck in a twenty-four-hour shift, which attests to how shorthanded they are. Supposedly, they'll be adding a full-time ER doc by next week, and our shifts will change to the promised four twelve-hour shifts.

Here's to hoping, because right now, I have an exhaustion headache from hell.

I review the case notes in the file for the next patient.

So far on my shift today, there hasn't been anything too major. One burst appendix requiring immediate surgery, one broken pinky toe, and someone coming in with a possum bite.

If they didn't want the possum to bite them, they shouldn't have picked it up. Of course, I couldn't quite say it that way to the patient.

ER doctors aren't known for their bedside manner, but we still have to draw the line somewhere.

I stop smiling at that particular memory when I realize whose name is on the paper. I hurry into the room where the patient is waiting.

"What in the world, Biff."

Hazel's dad smirks at me. "I didn't get a chance to talk to you this weekend, so I figured I'd come to visit you at your place of work."

I glance over the papers and raise my eyebrows at him. "You and I both know that's not true."

He shrugs and looks at the ceiling. Sure signs of guilt. "This says you came in thinking that you had a heart attack."

"All the technicians have said that my scans came back clear," Biff grumbles.

This is the man who, no questions asked, fixed the scrape on my dad's car after I opened the door against the mailbox. I'm pretty sure Dad doesn't know about that incident to this day. And to a young sixteen-year-old kid scared to lose his driving privileges, Biff was a hero in an oil-stained cape.

"They told me your list of symptoms, which is why I ordered the electrocardiogram." He definitely was not in here for nothing.

All the symptoms the triage nurse had listed to me

sounded like classic heart attack symptoms, although they were also symptoms of panic attacks.

Either way, it's better to be safe than sorry. So, I had them immediately get him connected for an ECG—not realizing that it was Biff.

I take a minute to review his chart and scan the results; then I look up at him with a grim set to my jaw.

This is the part of my job that will get interesting. Having to be an ER doctor to someone I know.

Someone who saw me do stupid stuff as a kid.

But knowing Biff as I do also gives me an advantage. So, I let him have it, knowing that he doesn't like to beat around the bush. "What are you doing stressing yourself out like this? Your body's shutting down on you." Most people of his generation don't take kindly to the words 'panic attack' at the outset. I have to ease them into it.

"What?" He frowns at me.

"You have way too much stress in your life right now. Otherwise, you wouldn't be sitting here."

"Well, when a guy has a heart attack, it tends to cause some stress." He chuckles, that easygoing laugh I heard so many times growing up.

I shake my head slowly, "Biff, you didn't have a heart attack. All the scans came back clear, but your body is telling you something. Your cortisol levels are probably sky-high. I'd like to run a blood test and run a full panel on those things if it's okay with you and get some answers that way. But all of your symptoms line up with a stress attack." *A few more explanations, and I'll be able to call it like it is—panic attack.*

He stares at me blankly, so I add, "Meaning that your body is telling you that you've had enough."

Biff studies the ground for a good minute before he looks up at me, "So I have too much stress in my life?"

"Yup. It induces a panic attack that feels exactly like a heart attack. You were smart to come in because whether it's a heart attack or a panic attack, some changes need to be made in your lifestyle."

I'm surprised when he doesn't immediately protest. Maybe he's already realized what I've been telling him, because instead of denying it, he asks, "But how do I make changes?"

I sigh and set down the papers on the counter next to me. I fold my arms across my chest and lean my hip against the counter. "What's going on?"

He opens his mouth to speak but then stops. He glances between me and the door as though we have an audience of eavesdroppers.

We don't.

I hold both hands up in the air and tell him, "I am under oath. I legally cannot share anything that you tell me in this room. Today I'm here to help *you*. Hazel will not hear a word of it from me." *Even if she needs to, unfortunately*, I think to myself.

Biff is stressed...and I wonder if Hazel is feeling the same way? Maybe her excuses for being busy were actually legitimate. It makes me want to find out exactly what's going on with her.

Biff nods once, "I've been trying to get this hip to heal so that I can get back to work. I've been doing office work, which I hate. Been dealing with customers, and that's been hard ever since Nicole died. You know how good she was with people. But now that I can't run the tow truck or do the tires, that's left Hazel to do that part. I've got a part-time employee that she's training as well. And now I'm the one left to run the office. I don't want to complain, because Hazel's been great. I can't think of anyone else I'd rather see running the business. But this dealing with people and customers thing? I don't want to get out of bed in the morning."

It's a lot to take in. Not the least of which is the fact that Hazel's been running the business—plus her own mechanic business on the side, and training a new employee. Maybe I *was* too hard on her, thinking she was trying to avoid me.

Maybe she's been busy working herself into an early grave.

My stomach turns at the thought. "Have you ever thought about retiring?"

He chuckles. "What would I do with myself? Besides, it's not like I can buy a mansion in Florida on my retirement."

Ironic, since I know he owns a cottage in Florida...I went there with the family before.

"How about a partial retirement?"

"Who would tow cars?"

"There are other tow companies in town..." I say quietly. "Maybe you could move to doing tires a couple of days a week."

Biff runs a hand through his gray hair. "It's true. And I know Hazel prefers the mechanic work to towing. I can't imagine what I would do with all my free time."

"Oh, I don't know. Take up a hobby. Golf. Lay on a beach. Go play cribbage at the Cataloochee coffee shop. Volunteer."

Biff actually looks as though he's contemplating it. "Truth be told, I've been thinking about retirement a lot lately. But I can't. Not yet, anyway. Plus, I've got other things to worry about."

"Like what?" I ask flatly.

"I've got the banquet dinner and everything to plan for that."

Aha. And now we're getting to the heart of the matter. Pun not intended.

The banquet. This year will be the tenth annual Harvest Hollow Cancer Research Benefit dinner.

Biff has made it one of the most memorable events of the year. I managed to make it back for the first seven but missed the last two. I don't plan on missing the tenth anniversary.

But planning a benefit dinner in your late wife's memory? That's a lot of stress. This is the first year Hazel's older sister Kara hasn't been here to help.

Biff says as much to me. "With Kara gone this year and Hazel busy taking care of the business, I've been handling all the planning. It seemed doable with Kara and Hazel's help. But doing it myself this year? It's been a lot. And it's always a hard time of year."

"Of course it is. Have you ever considered letting someone else manage it? You know the whole town is behind you on this. There are so many people grateful for the banquet and everything it stands for."

Biff nods. "It's crossed my mind. And honestly, this year is opening my eyes to the fact that I'm not getting younger. Maybe I do need to pass this on to someone else. It's just...hard."

Because letting go of the banquet would feel like letting

go of a part of his wife. I can't say that I blame him. Someday I hope to love someone as much as he loved his wife.

The man really needs a grief counselor, and that is not me. But I can do something to lift some of this stress off him and help Hazel as well.

"Unofficially, why don't you call me tomorrow morning when I'm off work, and we can talk about some simple steps to remove that stress."

Chapter 8

Hazel

I give the wrench a final turn, tightening the cable on the battery terminal. I pull out my voltage tester and rest it on the engine block, then walk around to start the car. Hopefully, this will do the trick.

The owner is going the cheap route and didn't want to replace the battery but rather recharge it.

The battery acid leaking out seems to suggest that it's time for a replacement, but they think I'm just trying to gouge them. I'll be putting my recommendation in big BOLD letters on their invoice.

Gah. It's actually been really nice having Dad handle the office part of the business. I get to do the towing, tires, and any mechanic work I can drum up.

I could work around the clock if I wanted, and sometimes I do. It keeps me from doing too much thinking. Because the more time I have to think, the more I realize I've put my dreams on hold. And that realization makes me slightly sick to my stomach.

I unwind the cords from the tester and lean over the battery.

"Oh, there you are!"

I bang my elbow on the hood. "Ouch!" I yelp another word that isn't as nice and turn to glare at the intruder in my shop.

Dark, messy hair, a little facial scruff and a t-shirt hugging a nice chest. How is he not freezing?

Tripp grimaces when he sees me grab my elbow. "I'm sorry. I should have been louder when I walked in."

"I'm going to have to attach a darn bell to you," I grumble. He must have slipped in the main door at the back. The large rolling door is still closed tight.

He holds out his hand, but I don't know what he wants.

I hold up the voltage reader, still in my hand.

"Not that, silly." He reaches past my extended hand and grabs my arm. He proceeds to gently massage my elbow and the arm muscles surrounding it. His warm hands distract me from the sharp pain, and pretty soon, my shoulders are sinking down limply.

He continues to massage up and down my arm, and I may or may not be desperately trying not to drool.

It feels amazing. I'll bang my other elbow if I get a massage like this.

The tingle flows all the way up my arm to the top of my head.

My eyelids start to feel heavy, and I wonder if I can nap standing up.

Tripp chuckles. "You've been working hard, haven't you?"

My eyes snap open, all thoughts of sleeping gone. "Working hard, or hardly working?"

He clicks his tongue. "You're starting to pick up sayings from your coffee group, aren't you?"

To my dismay, he releases my arm, and I feel as though I'm missing something. "I'll have you know I've learned several interesting sayings."

He looks at me with raised eyebrows and I decide to keep some of those classic sayings to myself. He doesn't deserve them.

Tripp turns to look at my rolling tool cart and picks up a tire iron from the top "Your dad called me this morning."

"At what time?" I stop next to him while I put the wrench away in the toolbox. I can feel the heat radiating off his body.

"Six a.m." Tripp answers with a quirk to his lips.

I can't help but chuckle. For some reason, my dad only ever calls people during the early morning hours. It's like his perverse pleasure in life to wake people up.

"He asked me to be your date."

I freeze, glad I'm not holding the wrench anymore because I might have dropped it on my foot. As it is, I barely catch the voltage meter by the wires.

"Just kidding. I wanted to see you get all embarrassed like you did when that woman thought I was proposing." He grins and dodges as I try to punch his arm.

A little friendly punch, of course. Not enough to cause any damage, but enough to leave a bruise. Possibly in the shape of five knuckles.

Ever since he's been back, he's been trying to embarrass me. "Tripp Vivien Sharpe."

His face shifts to playfully shocked. "Ohhhhh, so now I'm in trouble, huh?"

"If I have to pull out your middle name, you *know* you're

in trouble," I tell him as I tip my head up and do my best to glare down my nose at him. Hard to do when he's a lot taller.

"Not the middle name though," he groans.

Tripp's middle name was chosen to honor the doctor who figured out how to save babies with congenital heart failure. I was always a little jealous of that middle name. On the other hand, it seems to be the most thought Tripp's dad has given him. I definitely would not trade places with him for that.

Meanwhile, I'm named after a nut. Mom always told me it was because I was so sweet, but I know exactly what kind of a holy terror I was as a child.

"We're planning the benefit dinner." He drops the bomb like it's a food-poisoned burrito.

Plan the benefit dinner? There's nothing I want to do less.

Is someone's sewer backed up? Maybe I could help them. I know nothing about plumbing, but I am *willing* to learn.

Plan a benefit dinner? No. Not my expertise. That's in Kara's wheelhouse. In fact, maybe I could call her and get her to help...no, that's not fair. She's getting settled into her new job with her new husband in a new state. I can't ask my sister to come home and do this.

"Why are we doing this?" I whisper angrily. "You know I can't organize crap!"

There's a reason I've happily taken over Dad's part of the business while he heals. I don't want to be the one stuck in the house making phone calls and organizing a banquet.

"You organized street races." He has the nerve to hold up an index finger.

I press my lips together to stop myself from shouting. "That's different. It was high school kids blowing off steam."

"You organized a school-wide protest." His middle finger pops up to join the other one.

"They were going to cancel girls' volleyball." I fold my arms across my chest.

"You organize and run a business every day." He wiggles three fingers back and forth. I have the overwhelming urge to push them down.

I glare at him. "Don't you have somewhere else you could be?"

He smiles softly. "Listen. I know this time of year is hard."

"Understatement of the year," I reply. Losing your mom to cancer and then starting a benefit dinner in her memory is not on my list of easy things to work through.

He nods, and those stinking green eyes look at me warmly. "That's why I'm here."

I want to ask why he hasn't been here the other times. But that's not fair. He didn't have much choice with where he got sent for his internships. Arizona is a long way from North Carolina. And then after that, he took the first job that would have him as a resident: that had been in Oregon.

As much as I'd like to lay blame at his feet, I can't. But it would have been nice to have my best friend with me.

"Dad still doesn't have all of the auction stuff figured out," I admit. Now that I think about it, he hasn't gotten nearly as much of the stuff done as he promised. Apparently, Kara moving away has had a big impact on him as well. Yet another reason I can't leave him here by himself.

"Okay. We'll start with the auction then," Tripp says.

"I'll probably come up with something wildly inappropriate."

"I would expect nothing less." Tripp nods solemnly.

I blow a long slow breath out through my lips. It most likely makes me look like a horse, but I don't care. "Okay. I guess we're helping Dad. Did he say when he needed us to start?"

Tripp folds those nice biceps over his chest. "Are you free today?"

I look at the open hood trying to think of a way to get rid of him. Boredom. That'll work. "It will take me a while to finish up here. Give me an hour or so."

Chapter 9

Tripp

I'm beginning to think my suspicions aren't unfounded. Hazel *is* avoiding me. And I want to know why. Maybe I went too far embarrassing her at the Harvest Festival? I thought we were both having fun since she was the one who kissed my cheek—something I can recall in vivid detail, though I don't know why. But she seemed less than thrilled to turn around and find me here.

Maybe she needs to be alone.

Or maybe she needs someone to stick to her like glue.

So, instead of "giving" her an hour, I pull up an old metal bar stool and sit down. It feels nostalgic sitting here again. I used to spend hours sitting in this shop while I was in high school. I'd study for college entrance tests while Hazel practiced her skills on old beat-up cars.

Time to find out what's really going on. Whether it's work, stress, or—worst case scenario for me—she's outgrown our friendship.

She glances at me out of the corner of her eye. "This could be a while."

"I don't mind waiting." I make sure to grin at her as she gets to work on the car battery. While I'm not a car buff, I'm pretty sure she already finished whatever it was she was doing. She's stalling.

"Dad actually asked for help?" Her voice is muffled now that she's bent over the engine.

It's a shared trait between Hazel and Biff to never ask for help. How I answer her will determine how much she suspects, and I'm under oath to protect my patient's secrets. Even if that patient is my best friend's dad. "I offered."

She looks at me over her shoulder with shrewd eyes. Not much gets past her.

I give her the best excuse I can. "I know he had a hip replacement and that you've been covering for him. I figured the two of you could use an extra set of hands."

She presses her lips together flatly. "Can your hands pass me that plastic cover?" She points to the black hard plastic thing sitting on top of a table next to me.

I pick it up and carry it to her. "I'm not trying to encroach, Hazel. I know time changes things."

She freezes at that and slowly peers up at me as she takes the plastic cover from my hand.

"What changes?"

"Like you avoiding me." I swallow and try to force a smile on my face, but it's more of a grimace. *I went for the throat.* The uncomfortable realization I've been mulling over is out in the open. No more pretending. "Hazel, if you feel like our friendship isn't working any more, just tell me. I don't want to force you to hang out with me."

Hazel nods once. "Good. Because I don't really like being forced into things."

My heart takes a running leap then a swan dive directly for my toes.

Hazel turns her back to me and begins fitting the cover over the top of the battery. I wonder if this is the part where I'm supposed to leave and cry in an unmanly heap. I'm not above that.

Her voice trails back over her shoulder. "I *was* avoiding you."

I hold my breath.

"I was scared our friendship wouldn't be the same." She straightens and lowers the hood with a heavy thud.

She turns to face me as she slips her hands into the pockets of her coveralls.

"But then I saw you at the festival, and I realized we have the kind of friendship that stands the test of time." She smiles brightly at me. Those pouty pink lips stretch until her dimples show. Her bright blue eyes are twinkling. "I'm so glad nothing has changed."

I wouldn't go so far as to say nothing has changed, but I'm also not going to argue with the wave of relief I feel at her words.

She doesn't hate me.

We're friends. *And I really need to stop staring at her mouth and remembering the way her lips felt pressed against my cheek.*

"If it makes you feel any better, I was nervous to see you. It's been three years, and I guess I was scared we wouldn't hit it off after all this time—at least in person."

"Are you kidding? Who wouldn't love to hang out with me?" She grabs the front of her coveralls and points at a particularly large patch of grease. "Just look at me. I'm the picture of class. People are stumbling over themselves trying to be my best friend, but I have to tell them the position has already been filled."

And I will happily maintain that position for the rest of my life. "I'd be happy to review applications with you."

"Perfect. I was getting tired of trying to decide. You can do the interview process."

"Of course, they'll have to be willing to put up with some your dry sense of humor."

She sends a little pout my way.

It's different than I remember. After so many years together, I've seen her pout at many things. There was that time I refused to help her smuggle a llama into her backyard. Then there were all those times when she'd see me drinking coffee and want me to share a sip. Needless to say, I've seen Hazel pout quite regularly. It's her go-to combo with her puppy dog eyes.

She's always had full lips. It's been a joking point. I don't know why it seems so different today or why I can't seem to tear my eyes away from that mouth.

Stop creeping, Tripp.

"Just for that, you're being demoted to number two friend."

I clutch my chest as though it hurts—not too far off from the truth if she keeps staring at me like that. "Who's replacing me?"

"Annie Perkins, if you're not careful," she grumbles.

I roll my eyes toward the ceiling. "Finish up, Hazelnut. We have some planning to do."

She laughs and focuses on the task in front of her—whatever that may be.

Before I even have time to get bored, she says, "All done."

That was not even close to an hour long. I don't know what she was talking about.

She slams the hood, walks over to a sink in the corner of the shop, and washes off the remnants of grease. I watch in fascination as she slowly unzips the coveralls and slides them off. She's wearing a chunky sweater and jeans underneath.

I would be sweating working in all that, but it's not a heated shop. With winter fast approaching, it's getting a little chilly—and Hazel? She's always freezing. It could be seventy-five degrees and she would still need a sweatshirt.

Hazel kicks off her work boots and pulls a pair of tennis shoes out of a basket next to the sink. There are little flowers all over the shoes, and she slips them on without unlacing them.

She grabs the tie holding up her hair and pulls it out, letting blonde hair cascade down around her shoulders.

At about the same time she turns to face me, I realize I'm watching her in open-mouthed wonder.

I snap my jaw closed and smile uncomfortably. "That was quick."

"Oh, please. You know I'm always ready for anything."

"Even planning a benefit auction?"

She pokes my bicep as she walks by. "Now that, I might be mad about. I'll drive."

I snort. "*I'll* drive."

Chapter 10

Tripp

A s I pull into the downtown area, I realize the error of
my ways. It's farmer's market day. Which means
the downtown area is very crowded. I regret
choosing the Deep Dish for lunch, because hellooooo greasy
food, but I'm already dreaming about the pie. I can't change
my mind now. There's no going back.

"Farmer's market today," Hazel pipes up.

"Thanks, Captain Obvious."

"It's grown a lot in the last few years." She looks at me.
"You know we were voted the number two fall destination in
the US?"

"Number two, huh? Who took first?"

She scowls. "Some upstart in Vermont. Don't worry.
Harvest Hollow will take the lead next year."

There's the Hazel I know and love. So competitive, so
determined.

I freeze when I realize I used the word love in my own

mind. I haven't thought that about any of my girlfriends, but it's easy to admit to myself that I love my best friend. It's the kind of easy relationship I hope to find with someone someday.

"It seems like this whole town has grown a lot," I say as I struggle to find somewhere to park.

"It has, but it seems to be hanging on to its charm, don't you think?"

I look around at the shops, the fall décor lining the storefronts, then turn to Hazel and nod. "It's really a great town. I wasn't sure what it would be like coming back, but I'm happy to be here."

She smiles. "I'm glad. I was worried you weren't going to come back."

I reach a hand over and rest it on the back of her seat as I pull into the city parking lot and back into an empty spot. Guess I'll be paying a hefty fee today. "I've been a really crappy friend the past few years, haven't I?"

Hazel shrugs. "I think we've both been that way. We've been busy going to school, starting careers, and learning how to function in the real world. I have a retirement account now; doesn't that make me sound responsible?" she jokes.

"Yeah, but we hardly even called."

"But we texted. We sent reels and memes—which is the basis of every good friendship. And sometimes, we can only do what we can at certain stages of life. If we'd felt the pressure to call each other all the time, we'd be so annoyed." She laughs.

I smile. "You're right. In all the years I've been gone, I haven't met another friend like you, Hazelnut."

She bats her eyes at me and presses a hand beneath her chin. "That's because I'm special. My mom told me so."

"She was a hundred percent right. Now, do we dare walk through the farmers' market before lunch? Or will we spoil our appetite?"

"Definitely. I always find something I can't live without. Besides, I don't think you've seen it since it's gotten its own location."

"Wait, it's not at the Methodist church anymore?"

"Nope!" She unbuckles and climbs out of the car while I snap a picture of the number on the meter so I can pay on my phone.

"If you'll follow me, sir," Hazel says in a tour-guide voice, "I'll lead you to the Harvest Market Pavilion where you find all manner of local eats and treats."

"Don't quit your day job," I tell her as I trail slowly after Hazel toward the farmers' market set up with tents as far as the eye can see. It has grown so much since the last time I was here. The pavilion—is huge. I expected it to hold a handful of stands, but nope. It's crammed full of so many businesses I can't even count them.

"Does it feel like you're home now? Like you can settle down here?" Hazel asks as we pass a stand selling farm fresh eggs.

"It feels good to be back," I say hesitantly as I look at Candy Junction, a business I know has a brick-and-mortar store downtown.

"But not quite right," she adds for me.

I raise an eyebrow at her. Of course, she would pick up on my tone. Moving closer to dodge a mom with a double stroller, I explain, "It's just that I thought by now I'd have found someone to spend the rest of my life with. I thought when I came back to Harvest Hollow it would be to start a family here."

Hazel nods and waves to someone at a stand selling custom-made shoes.

"It's hard when life doesn't work out on the same timeline we expect it to," Hazel says, her tone sober. She pauses to look at a table selling jewelry. "All of your relationships fizzled out?"

"All three of them," I snort. "They were nice women, but it felt like something was lacking each time. And every time I hit the point of deciding if I should take it to the next level —I couldn't imagine spending my life with them. You know?"

"It's a big decision. I don't think it's something you go into without a lot of thought." She's so matter of fact about it. She doesn't have the outlook I do. The one where you're scared to repeat your parents' mistakes. Scared that maybe you are as much of a jerk as your father. Where you have a ridiculous hope that there's a soulmate for everyone.

"Do you suppose there's one person for everyone?" I dare to ask as we approach another stand. It's not one of our usual topics of conversation, so I'm not actually paying attention to the booths, which is a disservice to all of these vendors. I'll make it up to them next week. Right now, I need some Hazel-perspective to help me.

Hazel picks up a necklace and passes some cash to the woman sitting there. "Like soulmates?"

"Yeah, soulmates. I've always thought there was someone out there I was meant to be with, but now I'm not sure."

Hazel hands me her purse while she attaches the big

chunky necklace around her neck. She looks up at me with a curious expression.

"I firmly believe there are soulmates. But I think some people can be happy in life without marrying their soulmate, of course. There's a bigger spark, maybe more joy with your soul mate, though. I believe my parents were soulmates."

I nod. "I believe that too. I think that's what I keep hoping for but haven't found yet."

"You will. You're too incredible to miss. Whoever it is will find you. Granted, they'll have to be okay with blood and your fear of heights."

"Hey now," I say as I hurry after her, trying not to laugh. Only Hazel would know to insult me to pull me out of my bad mood. "I'm a catch."

"Hmm," she says as she looks at me suspiciously. "Yet here you are. Free and in the wild."

I lean down and wrap my arm around her shoulders. "You're making me want to do something very immature right now."

She throws back her head and laughs. "At least we know some things haven't changed. I'm still bringing out the worst in you."

"Come on, you menace. Let's go get lunch."

Chapter 11

Hazel

Apple pie for lunch for me—because pie is a full meal—while Tripp has a Reuben with pumpkin pie as a side. It's a solid choice.

"Okay, what about this? We sell tickets to next year's Harvest Festival." Tripp's been throwing out bad ideas like confetti. Dad told me that he needs items for the auction this year. With that being the main source of fundraising, we had better come up with something good.

I pause mid-bite. "You're joking, right? Those tickets are like three dollars, and it's a year away now."

"Listen, I'm just the bad-idea guy, here to witness your brilliance."

"Kara texted me a list of things she did last year, and she suggested that I don't put anything on the auction that's valued under $50. And that I should make it unique."

"She didn't have any good ideas though?"

I shove the last bite of pie in my mouth, taking my time swallowing before I answer him.

"*You* are notorious for good ideas," I remind him. He's thoughtful. To a fault. Beyond detailed. Everything has a backup plan. But today, he's decidedly *not* good at it.

"But maybe we need a bad one..." His eyebrows are doing that weird wiggle thing.

I narrow my eyes at him. "So, you're saying I have bad ideas?"

"I'm saying you have outlandish ideas. Ones that are unique and fun and might be exactly what someone would pay a lot of money for."

I lay my silverware across my plate in very precise motions so he can witness how civilized I am now. Too bad I see a smudge of grease that made it on my jeans. Dang it. These are my favorite. The waist is stretchy, so I don't have to unbutton when I sit down.

Hello, makers of pants; women like to sit down occasionally. Please remember this when sewing waistbands.

Meeting Tripp's teasing look, I say, "I think you're mixing up high school Hazel with adult Hazel."

"I also remember college Hazel..."

I bite my lip to keep from smiling.

That time we discovered just how fast my car could go...

But that does make me think of something. "We could sell tickets for a hot air balloon ride. Hanson has really turned it into a thing."

Tripp scrunches his eyebrows together. "Who's Hanson?"

"Oh, he's Annie Perkins's nephew. She introduced us and tried to set us up before."

Tripp frowns briefly, then takes a big bite of pumpkin pie. "Did it work?"

He has whipped cream on his lip, and I point to it.

He wipes it away with his napkin.

"Hanson's a fun guy. I enjoyed a coffee date with him, if you could call it that. We were both so busy that it was hard to connect. It wasn't like we weren't interested—it was more like I was busy working, and he was trying to *launch* his hot air balloon business."

Tripp looks at me flatly. "Please don't pun over lunch. My appetite can't handle it."

I smirk. "Anyway, Hanson wasn't like the guys I dated in college."

"Hmm, it's unfortunate they can't all be jerks like your college boyfriend."

I narrow my eyes. Dating Bret was not my most shining moment. "So, I made a mistake. Are you never going to let me live that down? I listened to you when it mattered, right?" I remind him.

Unfortunately for my boyfriend Bret, Tripp came to visit me during my sophomore year of college, and he did not like Bret at all. At first, I brushed it off as two young guys butting heads, but then Tripp sat me down and told me Bret was cheating on me with my roommate.

I confronted them both when I got back to my room after hanging out with Tripp.

Bret confessed and said he couldn't decide which one of us he wanted to keep.

I made the choice for him and never saw him again.

"I never liked Bret all that much," I confess. "But it seemed like a rite of passage to at least attempt to have a sort of serious boyfriend in college."

Tripp taps his thumb against the tabletop. "I'm beginning to think I'll never understand your dating requirements."

"Oh, it's very simple: there are none." I smile sweetly at him, knowing it drives him crazy.

"Okay, Miss Zero-Standards. Why don't you use that magical mind of yours to come up with something good to sell at the auction?"

I spin my water glass as I ask, "Do you really want me to get wild with this?"

Tripp studies me for a second, and then he nods. "Oh, yes. I want you to come up with something good. Something unique. That has never been done."

"Oh, I could come up with a lot of inappropriate things. Would that count?"

Tripp smirks. "I'm pretty sure I can come up with a few myself."

I really hope I'm not blushing as he says that. "Okay, how about this? We auction off dates."

He freezes. "What?"

"We. Auction. Off. Dates."

He stares at me for a second. "I'm glad you think you could actually auction off dates. But you already admitted that your schedule is full. How would you fit in all those dates?"

I snort. "Not me. We'd have several volunteers who are auctioning off a single date—with themselves."

Tripp rests his fist on the table as he leans back in his seat. "I think it could be interesting. But would you have people willing to do it?"

"I think if we put some very clear perimeters in place, it

could be a fun thing. There are a lot of young people in town. They'd enjoy doing it, I think."

"Are you sure it's not a little cheesy?"

"Of course it's cheesy. That's the beauty of it. It's so ridiculous that people won't be able to help themselves."

I lean my elbows on the table and stare at the crust left on his plate. "I'll have to think more about the details for a little while before I'll know for sure if it would work."

"You'll probably have it figured out by the time I get back from the restroom." He slides out of the booth but pauses to say, "Don't forget it's my turn to get the bill."

I wait for him to move past the booth, and then I hurry and grab my wallet out of my purse. I'll have to be quick while he's in the bathroom.

I slide the card out of my wallet and turn to wave to the server. The heck he'll get this bill...

The bench jolts as somebody slides in next to me.

I jump and slam back against the wall as I try to scoot away from the body sitting next to me now.

"Dang it, Tripp. Why'd you scare me like that!"

He flings an arm around my shoulder. "Because I knew you would try to pull a stunt like this."

He pins my arms to my sides and snags the credit card out of my hand.

"Let me take this for you."

I try to hang on, but he pulls it out of my hand with a quick jerk. He tosses it back in my purse and throws the wallet in after it.

"Give me that back." I try to reach for the card and wallet, but he's got a firm grip on me. There's nothing I can do.

"I told you that I was going to get the bill," Tripp tells me in a sing-song voice.

"You can't just bully your way into paying the bill," I chide. I'm painfully aware that grown-up-Tripp has more muscles than high-school-Tripp. His chest is rock hard but warm. His bicep is pressing against my cheek every time he shifts, reminding me that his arms are three times the size of mine now. While a friendly scuffle in high school *could* have ended with me winning, that's not the case anymore. I'm one hundred percent outclassed.

"Oh, but Hazel..." His voice is shaking with laughter. "I like to take care of my friends."

Our server is making his way toward us with concern in his eyes.

"Tripp, you're making a scene," I hiss.

"Is everything okay over here?" the server asks tentatively.

Tripp reaches over and smooshes my cheeks together with his free hand. "Everything okay, snookums?"

I do one of those ugly snort-laughs that live rent-free in your bank of embarrassing memories for the rest of your life.

Tripp lets go of my cheeks, and pretty soon, I'm gasping for air between the laughter.

"We're fighting over the bill," Tripp explains to the server.

"We are," I laughingly add. "I'm sorry. I can't bring him in public anymore."

The man's frown turns into a chuckle.

Tripp says, "She was trying to pay when I wasn't looking. But it's my turn to pay today."

Somehow, he manages to keep me tucked into his side *and* pull his wallet from his back pocket. He flips open his wallet, pulls out a card, and passes it to the server.

The server grins, relief on his face with the understanding that we're just joking around like children.

"Good grief, Tripp; you scared him."

He walks away and rings up the bill at the kiosk for us using Tripp's card.

I'll have to get even with him. Tripp smells amazing. And even though he's smudging my makeup against his very light-colored T-shirt, and I'm getting my face smashed against an armpit. Even that doesn't smell too bad.

I look up at Tripp's face, and he grins down at me. "You little sneak. You thought I wouldn't know what you were up to."

I try not to smile back, but I can't quite hold out against him. I poke his side. "Didn't you say you had to go to the bathroom?"

He raises his eyebrows. "I lied."

So matter of fact. Of course he lied. There are no morals involved in winning the bill battle.

His face goes serious, and he looks down at me. "I'm really grateful for your friendship, Hazel. I was worried about coming home. Worried that things would be different after all these years. But having you as a best friend? It's easy as pie."

There's a pain in my chest at his words. It's so nice. And so honest. Having him as a best friend *is* as easy as pie. Maybe that's something I need to get tattooed on me, to remind me.

Remind me that sniffing his deodorant is a bad idea.

With a heavy sigh, I wrap my arm around his waist and squeeze. "Thanks, bestie."

Chapter 12

Tripp

As Hazel and I leave the restaurant, she still has a smile on her face. Her eyes are twinkling, and she looks as if she's about to go out into the world and cause trouble. I love it when she has that look.

"Hey, do you want to go to the bookstore with me?"

She turns to stare at me with feigned shock. "When did you turn into a reader?"

"I haven't yet," I confess. "I'm still traumatized from medical school and all the forced reading I had to do. But I'd like to grab Mom a book. I'm going to visit my parents today. I don't want to show up empty-handed."

Hazel nods. "I've got the perfect book for her. Let's go. Do you mind walking? It's not too cold out today."

"I actually heard there was some snow in the forecast."

"Hmm, I still owe you for the last time we were in the snow together."

I step to the side to let a woman pass by. "Hey, if I recall, you were the one who started that snowball fight."

"Yes, but I wasn't the one who put snow down the back of my shirt."

"Nothing like holding a grudge for years..."

She turns and grins at me as she walks sideways. "I don't hold grudges, I get even."

"Of course you do." I laugh. Just then, she trips over an uneven part of the sidewalk. I latch on to her elbow.

"Oops, thank you. Oh look, the bookstore!"

Sure enough, we've arrived at Book Smart. I'd forgotten that it was so close to Deep Dish. Funny how spending years away warps your memory.

"Wait, something looks different." I pause and look up and down the street. My eyes land on a sign saying, 'Tequila Mockingbird.' "That. That wasn't always called that."

Hazel looks where I'm pointing. "That's right! Jolie McGraw moved back to town and bought the old Sullivan bar and renovated it then reopened it. It's great. They even have trivia nights."

"Jolie McGraw..." I shake my head. "I don't remember her."

"She was a tutor in high school. You probably never needed to talk to her," Hazel teases. "But I tell you what, she's made trivia nights fun."

I stare down at that blonde head. "Don't tell me you competed in Trivia with Aria..."

"I did not do trivia with Aria. I did it with Henry, Floyd, and Jean," she replies with a smirk.

"Now this I'm going to have to see sometime."

"You realize I have a killer memory, right? I just use it for useless information."

"I know you do, Hazelnut. Now, are we going book shopping or going to stare at a bar that's closed during daytime hours?"

Hazel straightens her coat, marches inside and takes a deep breath.

She and Mom have tossed book recommendations back and forth ever since high school when they discovered they both loved reading mysteries. I keep thinking I'll try one, but I wasn't joking when I said all the studying and late nights staying up reading to pass classes turned me off to reading...I would rather do anything else.

"There's no better smell," Hazel says with finality.

"Are you sure about that? Because I love the smell of freshly baked cinnamon rolls."

"Okay, but the thing is, here at Book Smart, I have the delicious smell of books and fresh ground coffee. It's like the best of both worlds. Coffee and books. I swear if they made a cologne that was that smell, men would have a lot easier time getting dates."

I look at her out of the corner of my eye and make my way to the mystery section. "I didn't know all it took for you was a good smell. I thought that a guy needed good looks and some toxic behavior."

She surprises me by flicking the back of my ear as she follows me. "It's not my fault men are awful."

"That's true. You really have had some bad luck—through no fault of your own." What kind of fool would date Hazel and leave her—or cheat on her? Yet that's what both her college boyfriends did. Bret was the jerk who cheated, but Mason—her senior-year boyfriend—was the one who decided he couldn't handle a capable woman. I'd had a long call with Hazel that night, reminding her that she deserved someone who appreciated all of her and didn't expect her to be less to make them feel better.

Hazel doesn't answer me; she simply focuses on perusing books. "Oh, look here! You need this one for your mom. She'll zip right through it."

She passes me a book I've never seen before, but I trust her. It's not like I've spent an inordinate amount of time in a bookstore.

"And this one. Maybe this one." She pats the top of a book she hands me. "I died laughing when they found the body."

"I'm deeply concerned about you," I say as she laughs and keeps finding books for my mom.

Soon, I'm worried I won't be able to see over the stack of books in my arms.

"Hazel?" someone asks from behind us. I turn faster than she does—curiosity killed the cat and all that. The voice belongs to a man wearing plaid shirt with a brown vest. He looks like he stepped out of Sexy-Woodcutters-R-Us.

I look at Hazel, who's smiling at him. "Hanson!"

He's smiling back at her like he's a man in a desert and he just found water.

I scowl. The coffee date man. If he was too busy to make time for her before, he doesn't get to do it now.

I nod in greeting at him and scoot a little closer to her, shifting the book stack to one arm the best I can.

He raises his arms and goes in for the hug. He's the same height as me, but the guy is built. Forget splitting wood, I'm pretty sure he throws logs before breakfast.

He envelops Hazel in a hug. Not like one of those sweet side hugs either—it's full-frontal assault.

She practically disappears, and I'm half-concerned I'll have to go rescue her.

"It's good to see you!" she exclaims when she steps back.

He smiles down at her. "You didn't answer my last text!"

"The one about going up in a brand-new hot air balloon? I figured I'd let you test it first, then give my answer." She laughs.

He doesn't look offended in the slightest. "You promise you'll come out and try?"

She nods once. "I think it sounds like fun."

I'm doing my best not to retch at her flirty eyes. Hanson finally turns to me. I stick out my free hand. "Hey there, I'm Tripp."

Hanson's eyes swivel to Hazel's.

"Tripp's my best friend," Hazel explains as she turns that bright smile on me.

Hanson relaxes his grip on my hand and now looks at me with less suspicion. Nothing makes a man more confident than knowing someone's been friend-zoned. And why does it bother me to be in the friend zone when that's what I am?

"Great to meet you," he finally says.

"Nice to meet you," I reply with a forced smile.

"Did you grow up in town here?"

"I did."

"That's great. I moved here a year ago. My aunt has lived here her whole life, and I fell in love with the place as a kid."

"Harvest Hollow is a special place, that's for sure," I tell him.

"Hey, I was just telling Tripp that I wanted to talk to you about something."

Hanson's eyes light up, and I hold my smile in, barely.

She did *not* just tell me that, but I have a pretty good idea what she's going to ask him.

"We're planning the annual benefit dinner for the cancer research fund. Lots of local businesses are donating things for the silent auction, and I was hoping I could talk you into donating an air balloon ride." She looks up at him with those big blue eyes as she explains.

Darn. I was hoping she was going to ask him to be one of the auction dates.

The stinker knows exactly how much this guy likes her—and she's not afraid to exploit it for the sake of charity.

"Of course! You can call me or come out to the place, and we'll figure out how to set it up," he replies warmly. He knows he's being suckered, and he's loving every minute of it.

I can't say I blame him. I've been scrambling to get Hazel's attention ever since I moved back to town.

Hazel waves a hand through the air. "Book Smart has donated several gift cards, which is great. It will be wonderful to do an auction this year. I think it will help local businesses a lot too. In the past, we've done ticketed seats, but this year we wanted it to be open to everyone and include more local businesses."

"Does this mean I won't get thrown out if I show up at the last minute?" Hanson asks as he leans slightly forward. How does Hazel not realize he's crowding her space?

"Well, it is a black-tie affair..." she whispers conspiratorially.

I clear my throat. I'm standing here, being a bookshelf, watching a lumberjack trying to flirt with my best friend. Nothing new.

Both of them ignore me. They keep throwing cutesy sayings back and forth. Flirty McGee.

So, I turn around and wander to the shelves. I spot a few of the titles that Hazel had mentioned wanting to read. I add them to my stack, then walk up to the counter to pay.

There's a young girl, maybe early college-age, working the counter. She pulls the stack toward her so she can ring them up. "Wow! That's going to be a big TBR."

"A what?"

"A TBR." She looks at me quizzically as if I'm the one making up words here.

"I don't know what that means."

She flips one book over to find the price. "It means to-be-read. It means you have lots of books to read if you want to make it through this stack."

I chuckle and explain, "They're not for me. I'm buying gifts."

"Well, whoever it is—they're lucky. I love it when people buy me books for my birthday."

"That's good to know. I'm not great at picking out gifts, so maybe I'll fall back on buying books."

"You literally can't go wrong with it."

I pass her my card, and she slides the books into a paper bag.

"Here you go."

I scoop up the bag and pocket the card. By the time I make it back to Hazel, the lumberjack is walking outside ahead of us.

"Well, did you get a date?" I tease her as I open the door.

"Hmmm, wouldn't you like to know, Mr. Nosy?" she says in a sing-song voice.

Yeah, I would. But I keep my mouth shut. "He seemed...handy."

Hazel nudges me. "You didn't seem to hit it off with him."

"I didn't have a chance to. You were too busy flirting for me to get a word in."

"Poor Trippy." She pats my arm as we walk around the block toward the parking lot.

When we get to my car and climb in, I open the paper sack and pull out the five books I bought for Hazel. I set them on her lap.

"Wait, these aren't the ones we got your mom, are they?" She flips them to look at their spines and then the back flap.

"Those are for you," I say as I start the car.

"What?" she practically shrieks as she looks at each one closer.

"You said you were wanting to read those and—" I don't get any more words out because she's leaped over the cupholders and is latched on to my neck—squeezing the life out of me.

"You're the best best friend anyone could have."

She smells like coconut and joy. Doing my best not to obviously sniff, I slip my arms around her and hug her back. "It's just books, Hazel."

"I know, but it was sweet of you to think of me. And to pay attention to what I was saying. I thought you were just humoring me in there."

She pulls back and I smile down at her. "*You* were the one helping me. I had no idea what to get Mom. Besides, I promise to always be honest with you, Hazel. And if I'm not paying attention to what you're saying, I'll tell you that I'm not interested."

She laughs and leans back in her seat. "Soooo, were you interested at lunch when I explained the way I replaced that cracked radiator?"

"No, not even remotely," I reply immediately.

She throws her head back and laughs loudly.

"Although I am impressed by how talented you are and your ability to repair things and diagnose the problem."

She reaches over and lightly punches my arm. "But that's exactly what you do. Only you're fixing people's bodies. And dealing with blood. Bleh. I could never."

I grin at that and back out of the parking lot. "Remember when you got a bloody nose during basketball?"

"Do I ever. They all thought I was dying. Turns out I don't like flowing blood. And is it really my fault? Blood is supposed to stay *inside* of you. If it's on the outside, you've got some serious problems going on."

"You've got a valid point there." I slow down as a truck and trailer pull onto the street, the truck bed loaded with pumpkins.

"Must be going to the farmers' market. But that reminds me, we need to go to Harvest Farms. They've offered to sell tickets and all manner of giveaways for the dinner. Dad talked to them, but he needs me to go out there and finalize the details."

"Is he driving the tow truck today?"

"No, Milo is."

"Milo?" A squirrel runs across the road and I have to swerve to miss him. He must live in the city park around the block. He's ventured a little too far from home.

"Milo Beecham is our new part-time employee," she explains as she flips open the book sitting on top.

"That's right. Your dad mentioned that. How's it going?"

She flips forward a few pages. "He hardly knew anything about cars or towing, but he's a quick study. I'm hoping Dad will hire him full-time. It'd give me more time to do some mechanic work."

"Hazel's Hot Wheels," I say with a smile. I pull into her long driveway and slow down to three miles per hour. She snaps the book closed and looks at me.

"You must be excited to visit your parents," Hazel pipes up, pointing at the speedometer.

I look at her out of the corner of my eye. "You know me a little too well."

"Any better?"

She means my relationship with Dad.

"I don't know. I kind of thought being an adult would make it better. But he seems to be getting worse with age."

Hazel drums her fingers against the stack of books. "You do know you're nothing like him, right?"

"Maybe his neglect is the best thing that could have happened to me." I turn to look at her.

No judgment. No telling me that my dad didn't "mean to neglect me." She's listening as I spill my guts and park the car.

"You know I support you no matter what. But I also want you to know you're an amazing person. I wouldn't change any part of you." She folds her arms and rests them on top of the book stack. "He'd be lucky to have a relationship with you."

I press my lips to keep from chuckling. At least I'll have Hazel to support me. And honestly? I don't think I could ask for a more loyal supporter.

Chapter 13

Hazel

I worry about Tripp as I watch him drive away. He might think he's over the way his dad treats him, but I know better. All I can do as his friend is remind him that he's a complete person the way he is; there's no need for him to change.

With a heavy sigh, I trudge across the gravel and pass by the shop door to the stairway that leads up the outside of the building. The stairs lead to my apartment, which sits above the shop. I hardly ever remember to lock it—which is good because I don't know where my keys are.

Dad probably has a spare key somewhere, but he won't remember where, either. When I walk inside, I kick my shoes off and toss them into my shoe basket. I walk across the thick, soft rug in my living room and flop down on the couch. My laptop is still sitting on the pillow beside me—right where I left it last night.

I have some invoices to write up and classwork to catch up on.

While my dad and his friends have been fantastic teachers, they didn't start working in the electronic era. So much of the repair work is electronic nowadays that I've been doubling down on some mechanic classes so I'll have a wider range of skills.

The best way I can learn right now is to take these online classes. Someday, I hope to work under someone who understands the systems well, especially since I'm more of a hands-on learner. But as of now, there aren't exactly a lot of knowledgeable mechanics floating around town. When people have problems with their cars, they take them back to their dealers in Asheville.

While I have built up a decent reputation in town, I can't offer full services—yet.

When I unlock the laptop, I automatically open my email to see if I have an answer from the mechanic teaching the class about a fried circuit board on an all-wheel drive hybrid.

Instead of the email I was looking for, I spied one from a Madge Cohen. Probably spam, but I open it anyway because those unread notifications bother me.

Dear Hazel Preston,

I'm reaching out to you to see if you would be available for an in-person interview and photo shoot with World Mechanic.

We are a company that specializes in all things automotive and are always looking for fresh faces to feature.

Adam Reeves recommended you to us.

If you would kindly email me or call (text would be even better) You can reach me here.

. . .

Sincerely,
   Madge Cohen
   Director of Operations
   World Mechanic

She attached her contact information and a link to her website.

So, like every paranoid crime show watcher, I open a private search tab and look up *World Mechanic* and search for their staff.

I've been known to read *World Mechanic*, and I've learned some things from their articles...but I want to see if this person is who she says she is. I'd like to know if she's about to ransom me for a million bucks that I don't have.

"Holy crap." I find a picture of Madge Cohen and her contact information is the same as the email.

Adam Reeves. Who the heck is Adam—

Oak Tree Adam. Why would he recommend me for this? I wonder what his connection to Madge is. Maybe they're in a relationship? That would make sense.

I hesitate for a few minutes, trying to decide how to proceed.

And ultimately decide it's worth the risk.

What harm could an interview with a popular company cause?

Maybe, just maybe, this is a way to move forward.

After tapping out a quick reply, I hesitate only a moment before hitting send.

I might definitely live to regret this.

And along the regretting line, I'm already regretting my date auction idea, so I sent a group text to Aria and Daisy. I went to school with Aria, and Daisy is Hanson's sister—a new-to-me friend, but so far, she seems great.

Hazel: What do you think of doing a silent auction for dates with people?

Aria: My teacher salary won't let me bid very high.

Daisy: I'm intrigued...tell me more.

Daisy has as much trouble with steady relationships as I do.

Hazel: I mean that YOU could be the dates.

Aria: Listen, if this is like the time you said ice skating on the pond would be fine...

Hazel: It was fine until Tripp toe-picked a little too hard.

Daisy: ? I wish I went to high school with y'all. I missed out on so much.

Hazel: Long story. I'll tell you next time I see you.

Aria: So, people will pay to go on dates with us?

Hazel: at a preselected, non-creepy, very public location.

Daisy: It sounds fun! Do you need more people?

Hazel: YES! I'm hoping to have between 8-10 people.

Daisy: I'll talk Hanson into it.

Aria: Please do.

. . .

I bust up laughing at that, knowing that Aria met Hanson at trivia night and told us that he improved the scenery.

But texting the girls has helped put my mind at ease. This will be fun.

Everything is going to be okay.

I have brilliant plans for the benefit dinner.

I have an interview with *World Mechanic*.

And I've firmly boxed Tripp into the friend zone in my mind.

Life is seeming much better. Downward spiral averted.

Chapter 14

Tripp

Funny that I assumed Hazel had been avoiding me, because I *know* I've been avoiding my dad. He's a little upset with me for having the audacity to be back in town working as an ER doctor. He still hasn't forgiven me for not becoming a heart surgeon. And to show up in town as "nothing special" is a flat-out embarrassment to him.

His words, not mine.

I turn down the street lined with historic Craftsman homes. These aren't the fun old homes that look like they've raised a few hundred neighborhood kids. No. These are the manicured-green-lawns, weeds-fear-for-their-life, and pressure-washers-are-used-every-Thursday type of homes.

Every house has a plaque hanging by the front door declaring the year it was built. Above the number, it holds the last name of the family that lives there.

When I find the Sharpe sign, I pull into the driveway and park a little bit crooked. It was something Hazel started when we were in high school. She liked to joke that no one in this neighborhood knew how to handle out-of-place objects. So, she purposefully parked her car crookedly.

Turns out she was right. One night my dad complained about her not knowing how to park correctly, and Hazel had busted up laughing.

If you look up the word "critical" in a dictionary, you'll find a picture of my dad there. I didn't aim high enough for him with my career in medicine.

Things have been even more strained since I decided not to follow in his footsteps and become a surgeon. I prefer the work of an ER doctor. Found that I loved the pressure that comes with it. The interaction with the patients, even.

The rewards and disappointments are both bigger. But I lack the same methodical coldness that my father has. And honestly, being able to separate himself entirely is probably what makes him a good surgeon. A trait that he sort of passed on to me. But I seem to save the emotion for later.

Dad also thinks my dream of having a family is an abhorrent waste of talent. I made the mistake of telling him in high school that I wanted to be a father someday. Heaven forbid that I dream of being a present father if I eventually have a child. My own dad wouldn't know much about that. Mom somehow carried the brunt of raising me, all while maintaining a dental practice in town.

My dad couldn't function without her, and I can't function around him.

There's still a part of me that longs for his approval for something I do. Or that he'll somehow wake up one day and realize his family matters. But pigs will probably fly before that happens.

I stall the inevitable passive-aggressive fight that's coming and sit in my car for a few minutes while I text my friend Archie Dunmore.

Tripp: How are you doing with Meyer? Has she threatened to hit you in the head again?

He texts back immediately.

Archie: Of course not. Don't be ridiculous. It's Meyer we're talking about.

I laugh and text back.

Tripp: you're right. Should probably have Willa go hit you on the head.

The friend group in Oregon is a tight-knit group, and I was lucky enough to be included while I was working there. Meyer is very sweet, with a fun sense of humor, but her friend Willa has a pretty spicy attitude, and seems willing to go to war for Meyer. If Archie steps out of line, he'd better watch his back with Willa.

Archie: How's life in North Carolina?

Tripp: Oh, it's going fine; I finally found Hazel.

He texts back as I shut off the car.

Archie: your best friend?

Tripp: Yes, my best friend.

He must not be working this evening because he pings back quickly.

Archie: I'm still not sure how I feel about that. I thought that we were best friends until you told me about her.

Tripp: Nothing personal, but Hazel has you beat by about 15 years.

Archie: Dang. Bring her out to Oregon, and we'll have a best friend competition.

Tripp: It's good to be back here, but I am missing Oregon. Maybe I can convince her to come with me.

Archie: I'll be planning the competition for when you do.

I tuck my phone into my pocket, climb out of the car and head inside to visit my parents. Both of them are sitting at the dining room table, eating an early dinner. It makes me extra glad I ate a late lunch with Hazel. If things get awkward with Dad, I can just leave. I won't feel the pressure to stay and sit through a meal with him.

"Aha, so you finally came home," Dad says as he sees me walk in the door.

I smile tensely. "Great to see you too."

Mom hurries over to greet me with a hug, and I pass the bag of books to her.

"Oh sweetie, you're so thoughtful." She pats my cheek like I'm still four years old, but I don't mind. "We have hardly seen you since you've been home."

Through every fault of my own.

Dad nods. "He's probably been hanging out with that Hazel girl."

I give up any pretense of trying to keep a smile on my face as I turn to stare him down.

"Don't you mean *woman*? She's not fourteen anymore."

Dad pulls out his phone to text someone while he answers, "She is still stuck here in this small town. Doesn't seem like she's done any growing up."

"Interesting observation for someone who is also living in the same small town." Despite living here for the entirety of my life, Dad has never appreciated Harvest Hollow the way Mom and I do.

I see Mom's lips twitching. I'm not sure if it's because she's about to laugh or if she's tired of us fighting already. But she jumps in to be the peacemaker as usual. "I really do worry about Hazel."

I look at her sharply. Dad has always been annoyed with my friendship with her, but Mom's always liked her.

So, if Mom says she's worried about her, maybe I should actually listen. "What has you worried, Mom?"

She sighs and sets down her fork. "I worry that maybe she *does* feel stuck here. She's had a lot on her shoulders."

I agree with my mom, but maybe she doesn't realize that's simply how Hazel is. She's always carried that family. She's been the thing that holds them together, especially through her mom's sickness and losing her mom. Hazel has kept it together.

Mom says again, "I worry that maybe Biff is holding her back."

"But she really does like the mechanical aspect of her work," I say.

"Of course she does. I'm sure she's very good at it, too," Mom says placatingly. "I'm saying that maybe—maybe she should have the opportunity to leave."

I narrow my eyes at Mom. "It's not like she's being chained here."

Dad snorts and just gets up and leaves the room, tired of our conversation about Hazel.

"Good visit," I mutter before I ignore him and turn back to Mom, who's still stuck on the topic of Hazel. Not surprising. Any conflict with Dad gets glossed over by my mother.

"Listen, sweetie, can you honestly say, in good

conscience, that if your father died you would leave me here in town by myself?"

I pause to think about it, and soon I see the same angle she's looking at it from. "You think she feels obligated to stay?"

Mom nods. "Maybe. She's such a sweet girl."

I shake my head. Yet again, another person says she's such a sweet girl. Not the kid I went to high school and college with.

"She's really just settled down ever since you left and taken care of her dad and her sister, taking care of the business, jumping in and filling in for any of the benefit dinners. But it's almost like I've slowly watched her lose her spark, especially after she was done with college," Mom muses.

Hazel had lived in the dorms the first two years then commuted the last two. I'd always assumed it was because she was homesick. But maybe she felt a different kind of pressure.

"I didn't realize you paid that much attention to her, Mom."

Mom shrugs. "Of course I pay attention. You two were practically glued at the hip for years. I've gotten attached to her. And I want the best for her."

Whatever the best may be. Unfortunately for me and my mother, it's not like we can force what we think is the best on Hazel. If she wants to stay in Harvest Hollow, I can't make her leave.

But then I'm left wondering, what if she doesn't want to stay?

Chapter 15

Hazel

L ast night, I stayed up way too late finishing the first mystery books that Tripp bought me. It's been way too long since I devoured a good book, and it feels like an addiction I can't stop now.

When I woke up this morning, I started the next one while I drank coffee. Forget that morning workout routine, I have four more mysteries to read. My home workout can wait until later. I sat and read four chapters while drinking coffee.

Unfortunately, adulting interrupted in the way of a flat tire on the side of the road, and since Dad was pretty tired after working yesterday, I had to answer the call.

By the time I get back to the shop, Milo is here and ready to work.

I get him set on changing the oil on a minivan, and now I have to talk to Dad about some questions I have on the logistics of the benefit dinner. I stare at the notebook as I trudge over to his house. I've done the walk so many times that I don't even have to look.

"Dad, why is there a blank page in the notebook with the word 'parking' on it?" I ask as I walk through Dad's front door. "Oh hey, Jean."

"Hi, Hazel."

Jean's sitting across from my dad at the kitchen table, drinking coffee and playing cribbage. A fairly regular sight.

"It says 'parking' because I haven't figured out the solution yet."

"Why don't we direct people to park in the city parking lot like we usually do?"

Dad sets down his coffee cup with a heavy thump. "Wayne Oakley."

"Ew."

"Hmm," Jean hums in agreement.

If Wayne Oakley were to decide to move to Arizona, about two-thirds of Harvest Hollow would help him pack. I'd offer to drive the moving truck. He can take any good thing and make it sour—it's his special gifting in life.

Dad continues, "He pushed it forward with the city council to make that metered parking twenty-four-seven. It's no longer free after business hours."

"You're joking. So, people are going to have to pay to park there?"

"Unless you can work a miracle."

I press my lips together. "Well, I'll march on down to City Hall and see what I can do about it."

"Uh, Hazel." Dad clears his throat.

"Yeah?"

"Don't go in there too mad, all right?"

"What gives you that idea?"

Jean interjects, "You broke the hard notebook cover."

I glance down at the three-ring binder. "Oops. Okay. I promise to calm down. But I also promise that I'll make him regret it."

With that, I spin around and head outside to climb into my car.

Metered parking my ass. This benefit dinner is for charity. I don't want more money lining Wayne Oakley's very large pockets. I have no doubt he's found some way to make the paid parking directly benefit him.

By the time I reach the downtown area—in record time, I might add, I've decided not to park in the metered lot ever again. Unfortunately, it means there will be some crisp walking in my immediate future.

The city park butts up next to the downtown area and they at least don't charge.

It's cold and brisk as I walk the couple blocks to city hall. Instead of cooling off my temper, it's turning it into a freeze-burning rage.

By the time I reach the front doors of city hall, it's raining. If I didn't know better, I would think my bad mood is channeling Elsa-esque powers.

"Hi, can I help you?" someone standing in the hall asks me. She has long red hair in a loose braid and is holding a tablet under her arm.

"Yes, I'm wondering who to speak with about the newly metered parking since we're running the benefit dinner after work hours, and they're still determined to charge for it, even though nowhere else does. I need to talk with Wayne Oakley since he's the one who pushed it through."

The poor woman looks taken aback, and I realize I just word-vomited the entire problem. It takes her a second before she nods. "Of course. We've run into this issue, and I'm actually working on doing some problem-solving." She glances around the empty entryway, as though she might get in trouble for saying too much. "I'm Elise, the city manager."

I move forward to shake her hand as she continues explaining in a quiet voice, "I'm doing everything I can to reverse that ruling. Even big cities offer a break on metered parking."

"I know, right?"

"If you want, you can submit a formal complaint." She sounds hopeful as she taps a pen against her tablet.

"Will that change what happens this month?"

Elise shakes her head. "Sadly, we won't be bringing up the parking issue again until November first."

I fold my arms and tap my fingers against my bicep. "So basically, I'm stuck with having people pay to park?"

"The city park has free parking!" she offers helpfully.

"I know. That's where I'm parked right now." I unfold my arms and glance around the room. "No chance of speaking to Wayne today?"

"He's busy harassing—I mean, he's out talking with some local business owners."

I smirk. "Well, I guess I'll have to come up with a better solution then."

"I'm sorry I couldn't help you," Elise apologizes, and she

seems sincere about it. "There really should be some better options."

"The street parking isn't metered overnight? They're still the old coin-operated ones."

Elise brightens. "No, they're not! You could at least have some people park there."

"At least that's a start. Unfortunately, we're expecting four hundred guests. In the meantime, I think I will try talking to Wayne if I can get a hold of him."

Elise hands me a paper and pen, and I can't figure out for the life of me where she had them hidden. "Write your name and number here. I can have him give you a call when he gets back. But he's been on a rampage lately about getting money out of tourists, so I'm not sure he'll have an open ear."

"What a grump."

Elise nods once and that's all I need to know I've followed up a dead end.

Chapter 16

Tripp

Today's shift has been relatively busy. Two car wrecks, a burst appendix, and a broken arm from someone climbing a rickety ladder to pick apples. The number of injuries we have during apple season is just disheartening. Have these people never heard of an apple picker? Or a ladder that doesn't have rusty rungs?

I shake my head and leave the room, taking the paperwork to the triage nurse. I pass off the folders and then make my way toward the room with the newest patient, who passed out unexpectedly. Based on case notes, it's most likely a blood pressure issue. I pause outside the door, and one of the charge nurses hurries over to speak with me.

Her name is Amanda or Alyssa or Amelia, and now I'm trying to get a glimpse of the name on her tag without her realizing it.

"Hi, are you on until seven tonight?" she asks right away.

"Yeah, I'm only doing a twelve today."

"Okay, well they say the new doc is coming in tomorrow," she whispers conspiratorially.

"Aha. Did you hear any specifics?"

Miss A shrugs. "I don't know. They say she has a lot of experience and that we were lucky to snag her."

"That's good," I say slowly. This woman looks nervous. "Are you worried?"

She shrugs. "Anytime a new doctor comes in it can change the dynamic. We all get a little nervous."

"That's understandable."

"But you were so nice right away, I'm really lucky to get to work with you." She smiles at me and that's when I realize that she might be meaning something more than professional.

Mercy General Hospital doesn't have a policy against staff dating each other...but I can't summon up the interest.

"That's nice. Everyone here has been competent and great to work with. Makes working here a great thing."

"I'm looking forward to getting to know you better!" she exclaims, then walks away when someone down the hall calls her name.

Carla. Not Amanda or Alyssa. Whoops.

I study the file notes one more time and formulate a few questions to ask as I walk inside the room. Time to solve a passing-out problem.

When I get home after work, I sit in my apartment and stare at the wall. There's no better way to decompress.

A car accident brought in a maternity patient and ended with a life flight to Knoxville.

Patty, who works weekends, texted me on my way home to tell me that both mother and baby were okay, but the baby would be in the NICU for at least a month.

Nothing prepares you for losing patients—or nearly losing them. Sometimes the relief can hit as hard as the grief. The times when you ask *what if*. What if I had decided to try and stabilize her at Mercy General, and then we lost the baby? Or what if we lost both of them? What if something had been wrong with the mother internally and she had died in flight?

What if I pursued Carla? She seemed like she'd be open to it. She's a good nurse. Pretty. Seems kind to the other staff. Why not ask her out?

Because I don't want to.

And therein lies the problem. I want a happily ever after, but I'm the one who keeps sabotaging it.

I keep thinking that maybe I'll *know* my person when I find them. Just like Hazel's parents. That maybe I do have a soulmate. But maybe I'm oblivious to her.

Hazel's optimism about there being soulmates gave me hope...but now I wonder if I've missed my chance.

I slip my phone out of my pocket and dial Hazel.

"Hazel's Hot Wheels, you've reached a recorded message. Please take your complaints and shove them—"

"Very funny," I shoot back. I can hear clanking in the background. "What are you doing? Replacing an engine?"

"Nope! I'm trying to make pumpkin bread."

"How's it going?"

"Well, it's going into the trash if you must know."

More clanking and an angry swear.

"Did you burn yourself?" I ask.

"Only a little one," she mumbles something else I can't hear.

"Do you need help?"

"No, I had this romanticized idea of sitting on my couch eating pumpkin bread while I read another book. Only half of that idea is going to work out."

I smile as I imagine her curling up with one of the mysteries I bought her. "Do you have a guess who did it?"

"Definitely the butler. It's always the butler," she teases.

I stand up and make my way to my small kitchen. I pulled out some pesto and pasta. "I haven't read enough mystery to know."

I pull out a pot while she tells me, "Well, then it's time to start. Your life will never be complete until you do."

Given my thoughts right before I called her, it's almost like she's poking at a wound. I stick the pot under the faucet, filling it to cook the pasta.

"Tripp. You there, buddy?"

There's a loud crash and I wonder if she threw the pan out her window. "I'm here."

She sighs. "What's wrong?"

"Nothing's wrong."

"Something's wrong."

I shut off the water and put it on the stove. "Bad day at work."

"I'm sorry, Tripp. Want to talk about it?"

"No." I turn, rustle around the cupboard, and find a lid for the pot. It's the wrong size. Furnished apartments aren't all they're cracked up to be.

"Want me to stay on the phone?"

"Yeah," I manage to say.

"Okay."

I hear a button beep and then she says, "Okay. I put you on speakerphone, and I'm trying one more time with the pumpkin bread."

She putters around her kitchen while I finish making my own dinner. She tells me all about the city parking issue and how she's hit a dead end. She complains about Wayne Oakley, the mayor, and anyone else attached to the issue. Then she starts giving me a play-by-play of how her pumpkin bread is turning out.

"I saw a house for sale on my way home tonight." Not quite true. I'd taken the long way back to my apartment. I needed some time to decompress and I had wandered through an older neighborhood at the edge of town. Bigger lots with modest but nice homes on them.

"Are you thinking about buying?" Something clinks on her end of the line.

"It's—well it's exactly the kind of house I could imagine raising a family in."

There's a soft clinking as though she's stirring her batter. "Is this an announcement?"

I sigh. "No, Hazelnut. No need to rub it in my face. I just think this place has a lot of potential. There's room for improvement, the price is right, and I like it."

"Whoa there, no need to get defensive about it. I was just making conversation."

"Ugh, you're right. I'm sorry."

"Text me the address so I can do a drive-by."

I open the link on my phone and send it to her.

"Oh, that is cute!" She makes a few other comments. "No shop though."

"If I ever end up needing a shop there will be plenty of room in the back acre to add one."

"Good point," she says as makes an extra loud thunk. "Dagnabbit."

"Okay, Bugs Bunny."

"It's really runny. Oh wait, I didn't mess it up!" she exclaims. "The batter tastes good!"

I pull my laptop out of my bag and set it on the counter. "I have a friend in Oregon, Margaret. She could bake some pretty amazing stuff. I might have to fly you out there so you can learn from her."

"Your friend Margaret? As in like a girlfriend?"

"Despite her best efforts, I never did ask her out..." I pause for dramatic effect. "She's in her 80s. She's tons of fun, but you know—just not the *one*."

It takes Hazel a minute to catch her breath from laughing so much. She takes a few deep breaths before responding. "You know, I think that sounds like fun."

"What sounds like fun?"

"Going to Oregon with you."

I hadn't expected her to agree. She never leaves Harvest Hollow. And it makes me wonder if my mom is right. If maybe Hazel's too afraid to leave her dad. Losing a parent in high school does a number on you, and I see the way it's affected Hazel and Biff. Kara too, in her own way, but she seems to have been able to move forward with her life. Biff and Hazel are frozen in time.

"Let's do it."

"What?" she asks as she turns the faucet on.

"Go to Oregon." I open a tab on the computer to search for tickets but pause when I see my dirty dishes on the stove still.

She laughs. "How silly. Did you forget that I'm busy working? That *you're* busy working?"

"No, I didn't forget; I thought we could plan a weekend trip. I want you to see Oregon. I think you would enjoy it. Plus, you'd get to meet Archie and Meyer. I think you might like that."

"I think you're off your rocker. We have a benefit dinner coming up. I can't just leave."

"Fine. After the benefit dinner then."

I throw the pot in the sink and put the jar of pesto away.

"I want to. But I'm not sure if I can," she admits. "I've got a lot going on."

"Okay, we'll plan it for a time when you're not as busy."

"It's a deal."

I flop down onto the modern-style couch that might as well have been made out of concrete. "Thanks, Hazel."

"For saying I'll go to Oregon with you?"

"No. For being there for me. You always have been. And I know we suck at telling each other emotional things, but you mean the world to me. You're the first person I call or text when I'm in trouble."

"Yeah, about that. Maybe you could start living a charmed life or something," she teases.

"Very funny."

She clears her throat. "It's okay, Tripp. I'm happy to be there for you. Lord knows you scraped me off the floor countless times when Mom passed away. I'll never forget that."

We sit in silence together for a minute. "Hazel."

"Yes?"

"There's a spider on my ceiling."

She snort-laughs. "Be a big boy and get it."

"Ugh, I was afraid you'd say something like that." I stand up and size up the spider situation. I'm gonna need a ladder and full-body gear. It looks big. "What are you doing tomorrow? Coming to help me not get eaten by spiders?"

"I've got a few tire appointments tomorrow. Milo's working, so I'll be there keeping an eye on how it goes."

"Suppose your dad can supervise while we go do something fun?"

She hesitates a minute. "Let me talk to him, see what he has going on. I'll text you."

She hangs up and texts me ten minutes later.

Hazel: We better have the most fun you could ever plan. I haven't had a full day off in a looooong time.

Chapter 17

Hazel

I have a voicemail on my phone the first thing in the morning. Wayne Oakley is attempting to ruin my day off. Bless his heart—and not in the nice way.

The message sounds way too cheerful at this time in the morning. "Hello, I heard about your complaint from Elise, and I'm sorry to tell you, city policy will not be changing at this time."

Wayne did not sound sorry. He sounded smug. "You're welcome to email suggestions to me or Elise and we'll consider bringing them up at the next city council meeting."

Maybe I should go to the mayor with this. Though I don't think he would be any better.

One very short hour later, Tripp is standing at the top of my stairs, dressed in my worst nightmare outfit. When I told him last night that he better come up with something fun to do, I didn't expect to be disappointed.

Yet here he is wearing hiking boots, a baseball cap, and a jacket. I shouldn't have opened my front door.

"We're going hiking."

The hell we are. But instead, I smile at him. "What a crazy idea."

"Put your boots on."

"No." I turn around and head toward the kitchen in my apartment. "When you said fun last night, I pictured you bringing apple fritters and us bingeing Ted Lasso on the couch."

Tripp follows me inside. "Hazel, the only time you've left home in the last month is to tow a broken-down car."

"I actually go to the coffee shop regularly." I open the bread bag that's holding the leftover pumpkin loaf that turned out well the second time.

"Of course you do." He sighs as though I'm the most trying thing he's witnessed this week.

But I know better. I heard that Floyd's grandson—age twenty—went to the ER this week because he ate a peanut butter sandwich, knowing he was deathly allergic to peanuts. Word is, he assumed he'd outgrown the allergy.

I have a feeling that whatever Tripp was calling about last night was even more serious than that, though.

"Hazel. You need fresh air." He plants his hands on his hips and looks at me sternly.

"You mean breathing in diesel exhaust doesn't count?"

"Just a little hike. Please."

I turn around and stare him down. He's giving me his best puppy dog stare. And it's working.

"A little one, right?"

"Yes, only a little one."

I shove as much pumpkin bread in my mouth as I can fit. Tripp's eyes widen slightly.

"Geez, Hazel, trying to choke?"

I swallow and shake my head, sending a ghastly amount of crumbs flying off my lips. "If a prisoner only gets one final meal, I'm going to make it count."

Tripp throws back his head and laughs. "I'm not taking you to prison; I'm taking you hiking."

He walks over to me and grasps my shoulders, his hands warm and firm as he turns me and marches me down the short hallway to my bedroom. "Find something warm and some good hiking shoes. I'll buy you an apple fritter on the way out of town."

I glare at him over my shoulder. "Promise?"

He crosses his heart. "Promise."

I point at him in an empty threat.

"Okay, Hazelnut. It'll be fun! Now, can I try that pumpkin bread on the counter?"

"If you dare." I slam the door and hurry to change into some fleece-lined yoga pants. He said to find something warm, and I'm taking his advice. "Hey, what happened with the spider situation?"

I can hear creaking in the kitchen. He's standing by the sink, I can tell. The floorboard always squeaks whenever someone stands there.

"I think I won, but I'm not sure."

I pull out a thick sweater and jerk it on over my sports bra. "How can you not be sure?"

"When I climbed on to the chair to get it, it fell down my shirt, so I threw the shirt outside!"

I grab the pair of hiking boots Dad got me ten years ago. Practically brand new, for all the hiking I do.

"But wouldn't that be in your apartment building hallway?" I ask as I walk into the kitchen to see him finishing off the last of the pumpkin bread.

He looks at me guiltily. "I threw it out the window."

I can't help but laugh. I've only driven by his apartment building, which borders the downtown area and the start of the business district. His apartment window is directly above the side street. "Did it land on someone unsuspecting?"

I squat down to lace up my boots.

"I was too scared to look," Tripp admits as he washes his hands. "You look ready. Let's go."

"If you think I'm going to hike a long way without an apple fritter..." I let the unfinished threat hang in the air.

"I promised, didn't I? Besides, it will be a short hike."

Chapter 18

Hazel

We drove all the way to the Blue Ridge Mountains. (Tripp did make good on his donut promise though, so at least I have some carbs to do this on.)

His little hike is not looking so little when he starts throwing water bottles and a first aid kit into a small hiking backpack.

"What's wrong with you?" That is not a small hike he's prepping for.

"It's going to be fun!" He looks up at me and grins as he keeps filling the backpack.

"You need to learn how to have fun. I knew I shouldn't have trusted you with this." I fold my arms over my chest and do my best to glare at him.

He looks crestfallen, and I'm pretty sure I just inserted my entire foot into my mouth. My stomach lurches as I realize this really is special to him.

Tripp grew up with exacting parents. High expectations.

I'm the one who dragged him into fun. Forced him to loosen up. He's always had a hard time letting go with people, or even figuring out what fun was. If hiking is what he considers fun, then I'll play along. (Just this once.)

I sigh. "Fine. We will have fun on this hike, but I reserve the right to whine and complain and possibly make you carry me at some point."

He grins. "It's a deal."

I smile as best I can, but I don't fool him. Tripp throws back his head and laughs. "Listen, it's only a four-and-a-half-mile loop."

My mouth drops open. He reaches a hand out and pushes my jaw closed again, his fingers grasping my chin.

"You look like a fish," he says.

I scowl at him.

"A cute, angry fish. Come on. Let's go."

"I might die."

"You could literally pick me up off the ground right now and probably throw me, but going on a short walk scares you?"

I glare at him. "You're a merciless tease. And a bully. Yes, that's exactly what you are, a big giant bully."

"I'm saving your heart health."

Oh boy how he does not know what he's doing to my heart. Because I can still feel those fingers against my skin even though they're gone.

"Why don't you lead the way?" Tripp suggests. "We're not out to set records, just have fun and enjoy ourselves."

Tripp is setting records. The man is on a speed hike. He must be training for the Olympics or something because when we hit a fork in the trail, I asked him to lead. He took off for that trail like a bear was chasing him.

I wish I'd gone shopping with the girls. Or that dad hadn't agreed so quickly to help Milo.

Literally anything sounds better than this lung-burning experience.

"I can't go on another step. Go on without me. I'll be fine. I'll catch you at Christmas." I gasp as I rest my hands on my knees.

Tripp has gotten mean in his old age because he laughs and grabs my arm, dragging me after him.

"I can still see the car. We keep hiking. Good grief, Hazel. You used to play every sport there is. I watch you lift ridiculously heavy things in the shop. A little walk shouldn't be killing you."

"Easy for you to say. I probably haven't done cardio since college."

He looks at me sternly. "Good thing I'm here to look after your health. Come on."

"Cruel man."

By the time we reach the one-mile mark, I'm thinking about turning around; Tripp's firm grasp on my hand removes that option.

By mile two, I'm contemplating digging a shallow grave for Tripp and being done with this madness.

Two things stop me:

1) the fact that I don't have a shovel.

2) I'm so out of breath I don't think I could operate the shovel.

"That's it. We're going on hikes every week until your lung capacity builds up."

"I'll flee the country," I gasp.

Tripp chuckles. "First, you'll have to flee the county."

I glare at him until he stops. "Want to rest a second?"

I don't even bother to answer him as I collapse to the ground. "You're evil. Horrible. Treacherous. You LIED. You told me that this was an easy hike. I tried to make it fun."

"It is. I hiked several mountains in Oregon that were much steeper than this."

"I don't believe you."

"The Blue Ridge Mountains are a gorgeous, beginner-friendly place to start. If I'm going to bring you out to Oregon with me, then I've got to get you in hiking shape."

My heart catches, and I don't know if it's because I'm about to die or if it's the thought that Tripp wants to bring me with him. It took me by surprise when he threw that question at me last night. Maybe because it's something I'd actually like to do.

I lay flat on my back on the trail. The leaves crunch under my head, and I know I'm getting dirt in my hair. I stare up at the sky through the tops of the trees. "You mean to tell me that you would drag me across the United States and force me to hike? Whatever happened to vacations where you lay on a beach and sip margaritas?"

I hear Tripp laugh. "Trust me, you don't want to lay out on an Oregon beach and sip a margarita. A hot coffee, maybe. But not a margarita."

I grin at that, and I can finally feel my heart returning to a reasonable pace.

I feel a nice breeze on my face, and I'm deeply regretting

wearing a heavy cable-knit sweater. I'd love nothing more than to peel it off right now. Too bad I'm not wearing anything underneath besides a bra.

"Tripp."

"Yes?" he asks as he sinks down to sit on a log next to my prone form.

"It's really pretty here. And peaceful. Thanks for bringing me."

"Any time, Hazelnut."

We rest a few more minutes, and then Tripp leans down to grab both my hands. He stands over me and bends down to pull a leaf from my hair. "Sorry, I took off too fast. Sometimes hiking is how I blow off some steam."

"I figured." I gasp as he pulls me all the way to my feet. Zero effort is required on my part. He turns me around and brushes the dirt and leaves off my back and legs.

"Thank you."

His hands rest on my shoulders, and he squeezes gently. "Better?"

I look back at him and bump against his baseball cap. "All better. Ready to hike ten miles. It'll be easy as pie."

He drapes an arm around my shoulders and pulls me with him as we start down the trail. "Whenever you say that...it means the complete opposite."

I nudge his ribs with my elbows. "Don't pry too much. You might not know what I'm really thinking."

When we take the wrong turn and add two miles to our hike? I let Tripp know exactly what I'm thinking.

Chapter 19

Tripp

Hazel's ability to complain while hiking is unsurpassed. She keeps saying that I'm in shape, but the reality is, if I tried to talk half as much as she is, then I'd be lying on the ground next to her. Yup. She's lying there again.

"Leave me here. Bury me on this hill. Don't even bother with a grave marker. You'll never find me again anyway. It's too far away."

She throws her arm over her eyes as if she's some historical femme fatale who drank the poison.

I bend down and rest two fingers against her neck. Her pulse beats steadily and about the same pace as mine. She moves her arm and glares at me. "Good grief. I'm not dead yet."

"Just making sure you're being a drama queen."

"I resent that remark," she snaps back. But I spot the smile before she hides it with her arm.

I pick up a pinecone and throw it at her lightly. It bounces off her leg.

She sits up with a gasp. "Tripp Sharpe. You didn't."

I grin at her. "Come on, slow poke."

I turn around to head up the trail but stop the second something smacks my back. I turn around to find Hazel standing there looking intently at the sky, whistling a tune as though she wasn't the one who hurled a pinecone at my back.

Her eyes are sparkling, and she has that carefree air about her. And I realize something. I'm having more fun dragging Hazel on a hike than I have on any of my dates in the past three years.

"Hazelnut. You didn't."

She looks at me with wide eyes. "Didn't what?"

I bend down and pick up a pinecone, throwing it at her legs. She jumps to the side and barely dodges it. Then returns fire, pelting my thigh with what feels like a rocket.

"Ouch!"

She flings them at me as fast as she can pick them up. I move closer until I can wrap her in a bear hug from behind, pinning her arms to her chest.

We're both laughing and breathless.

"Are you going to be good?" I ask as I move her hair out of her face.

"Probably not," she admits with a laugh.

"I guess we'll have to stay like this then," I sigh as though I'm not having fun and drag her backward to sit on another fallen tree. She's still trapped on my lap and laughing.

"You started the pinecone war."

"You're supposed to be tired from hiking," I remind her as her whole body shakes with laughter.

"I can't help it! If you start a pinecone war, I'm physically compelled to finish it."

"But you don't feel the same about hiking?" I ask.

She leans back against my shoulder and looks up at me. "Not in the slightest."

She grins, and those bright white teeth practically sparkle against her soft pink lips.

"You smell good," she says as she looks up at me. And then she takes a long sniff. Full-on plants her face against my neck and sniffs.

The strangest sensation comes over me to return the favor. I want to lean down and bury my face in her soft hair. Find out if it's her shampoo that smells like coconut or her perfume.

My chest starts burning from the inside, and I know it's not the beginning of a heart attack.

Heck.

I'm attracted to Hazel.

It's not a fluke like I'd hoped.

I'm in deep trouble.

Chapter 20

Hazel

By the time we get back to my place, I'm dreaming about lunch. And despite my hunger, I know I can't go to a restaurant covered in dirt and leaves. The first time I laid down on the trail was not the last. We had some good laughs over the wrong turn.

Tripp's was a more good-natured laugh. Mine was more along the lines of an I'm-going-to-murder-you laugh.

"Did you have fun?" Tripp asks as we pull into the driveway.

"As much as it pains me to admit it...yes, I did. But now you have to feed me."

His eyes land on my mouth and stay there a moment.

"What?" I ask.

"Just quickly calculating if my credit card can take it," he says as he blushes.

Safe to say that is not what he was thinking as he looked at me.

"Okayyyy. Well, I'm going to run upstairs and take a quick shower. Want to come wait inside?"

He shifts the car into park, keeping his focus out the window. "Maybe I'll go see if your dad is at the shop."

"Okay, sounds great! I'll be up there roasting my skin off in a hot shower. I'll be out in a little bit."

I run upstairs but take my time in the shower. The shower is my thinking spot, and boy do I have a lot of thinking to do. Am I imagining Tripp staring at me more than normal? Am I imagining him making up excuses to be close to me? To touch me? Maybe it's my own fantasy trying to find a foothold and it has nothing to do with him.

"Whatever it is, he better fish or cut bait," I mutter as I shut off the hot water. I can't take the yoyo of emotions he's sending me on.

I throw on my T-shirt and overalls, along with my floral tennis shoes. They say it's a major faux pas to wear bright colors in the fall...but it's one rule I happily break.

I grab a beanie, throw it on over my wet hair, and hurry downstairs to see if Tripp found Dad or not.

When I walk into the shop, I find Dad, Tripp, and Milo standing around the coffee machine. No one is working.

"Hey, I see what happens when I leave! Nothing gets done," I tease.

Milo jumps as if he's about to go back to work, but Dad rests a hand on his shoulder. "She's joking, kid. Besides, you've solved all our problems."

"What's the problem?" I ask warily.

Tripp pipes up, "The parking problem. You were worried about people not having enough room to park, or not realizing city parking is twenty-four-hour regulated..."

"Yes, I seem to remember complaining about that problem..."

"Well, Milo is your solution." Tripp holds out a hand toward him.

"How so?"

Milo shifts back and forth on his feet. "Before I moved to Harvest Hollow, I worked with a valet service in Knoxville. They travel all around the surrounding areas. What if you hired them to help take care of the parking issue?"

All three of them look at me with hopeful smiles. "That —might actually work! The city park has free parking and is only a couple blocks away. It would be the perfect spot for the cars."

"See? Problem solved. And you didn't even have to stress about it." Tripp folds his arms across his chest in a challenge. It's a good thing there's an audience, because otherwise, I would be tempted to wipe that smirk off of his face.

"Do you mind giving me their contact information, Milo?" I ask as I move to stand next to Tripp.

"Sure thing, I can text them too and make sure they do it." He smiles brightly and I'm beginning to think there's hope for him after all.

"Perfect." I elbow Tripp. "Now you owe me lunch. You guys got lunch plans?"

"Yup. Going to pull a truck full of pumpkins out of the ditch," Dad answers.

"Are you sure you don't want me to—"

"I'm fine!" Dad shoots back. "Stop your worrying."

Right. Because that's the immediate cure to stop worrying. "But what if you—"

I don't get to say anything else because Tripp picks me up under my arms and carries me out the door.

"Do you know you are getting into this bad habit of carrying me places?"

"I have to admit it's kind of fun. And a lot quicker than waiting on you."

I turn around and poke his bicep. "One of these days, I'll pick you up and move you along faster."

"It's for your own good. I'm taking you to DeLucca's for lunch."

That freezes any argument I had saved up. "Breadsticks. Alfredo."

Tripp nods and points to the car. "Let's go!"

Chapter 21

Tripp

I t's been four days since the hiking incident, and I still haven't stopped laughing at Hazel's creative death threats. Unfortunately, that's not the only thing occupying my mind. There's a frozen image of me holding Hazel in my arms, staring down at her and not wanting to let go.

Luckily, I worked three days in a row, and Hazel's been busy in her shop, so I've had some time away to remind myself that Hazel is my best friend. That I'm in a dry spell and it's only natural to be *sort of* attracted to a drop-dead-gorgeous woman.

Today we're meeting at the coffee shop to review our plans for the benefit dinner. Biff is still doing a lot of the work, but we're working out the parking and auction items. And we're getting down to the wire.

When I walk into the shop, I spot Hazel standing at the coffee shop counter, waiting for the barista to hand her a mocha.

The coffee shop is fairly busy, and enough conversations

are happening to make it difficult to find a quiet spot to sit and talk with her. I assumed I would beat her here because she's always late. Which is why I packed my laptop so that I could start the process of scouting out any new job openings. Now that they have one long-term position filled, the local hospital has said it will be posting another position soon.

What's worse is I don't know what I want. Do I want a full-time position in Harvest Hollow? Do I want to try and go back to Oregon? Do I apply somewhere I've never been? The only thing holding me in Harvest Hollow is Hazel. For some reason, it hurts to think about leaving her again. She's been my anchor—more than my family has.

I don't know if I was meant to settle down in Harvest Hollow or not. All I know is that it's good to be back. I end up choosing the table by the big bay window, and even though it's surrounded by people, it at least has a plug-in under the table.

Hazel doesn't realize I'm here yet, but that's okay. I'll save the one open table for us. I pull open my laptop and glance back at Hazel. She's wearing high-heeled boots with some kind of sweater dress thing that cuts off mid-thigh.

There's a gap between the boots and the sweater where I can see nicely toned legs. How does she have tanned legs in the middle of fall? They look good on her. And I don't like to think about why I think they look good.

What on earth. *Tripp, get a hold of yourself. This is your best friend. You can't be thinking about her tanned legs.* I clear my throat and open my computer.

Right.

Work. Work. Work. That's all I should be focusing on right now.

She picks up her coffee cup and takes a slow sip from it. She starts to turn, and I lift my hand to catch her attention. A man walks up to her before she can do a full scan of the room, and he stops next to her.

I don't recognize him. He's somewhere around our age.

In his late twenties, possibly early thirties, and Hazel smiles when he speaks to her. She must know him somehow. And there's something uncomfortable about her having friends that I don't know about. At least with Flirty-McFlirty Hanson, she'd told me about him. Is this someone else she's dated? Or is hoping to date?

I shake my head at myself, knowing that this is ridiculous. I try to focus on my laptop, but then my ears start picking up pieces of the conversation.

Words like "dinner, lunch, busy?"

With a grunt, I close my laptop, stand up and make my way to Hazel. I can't hear the conversation from all the way across the room.

Their words are mingling with everyone else's.

I slowly move closer, dodging around a woman that's helping a child carry hot chocolate to the table. Hazel's eyes widen in surprise when she notices me.

"Oh, hi Tripp, I didn't know you were already here," She smiles briefly at me, then turns back to whatever dingdong this is.

The man glances at me and studies me for a second before he turns back to Hazel, "I hadn't realized you were here on a date."

"I'm not." Hazel laughs, her cheeks turning pink. "This is Tripp. He grew up in Harvest Hollow."

She didn't introduce me as her best friend. I don't know

what that means, but I definitely take note of it. I've somehow changed labels since she introduced me to Hanson.

The man smiles at her, and I don't like the confident look in his eyes. "Of course. I'm so new to town and learning names and faces. I know a lot of you are lifers here."

Hazel nods. "Yup. Born and raised, isn't that right, Tripp?"

Don't drag me into this conversation, I try to convey telepathically, but she either chooses to ignore me or is deciding I've earned it since I did walk over here of my own free will.

"That's right. Although the town is big enough that I never knew everyone, even growing up here."

The man nods. "I moved to town a couple of days ago, and Hazel had to come to rescue me on the side of the road when I had some engine trouble."

He grins at her. Grins as though he's completely comfortable with being rescued by a woman. I hate how I'm already liking this guy. I've always had a hard time with anyone who made snide comments to Hazel about her job. Treated her as if she's less-than because she's not performing a gender-typical job. And this guy in here is smiling and flirting with her and accepting her as she is...why does this make me uncomfortable?

Chapter 22

Hazel

Why is Tripp glaring at Adam? For that matter, why is he glaring at me?

Chapter 23

Tripp

"So, Friday night for the date?" the man asks.

"Friday should work—" Hazel starts to say with a big smile pointed right at him. She has both dimples showing, and her eyes are twinkling. The guy is a goner. You can't help but get pulled in by Hazel's blue eyes.

"Did you forget you have something going on Friday?" I don't know why I asked that. I'm going off-script. Off the best friend script.

Hazel looks at me with a strange—and dangerous—look in her eyes.

"It doesn't matter."

"Umm, actually, it does." I chuckle because there's no way in hell I'm letting her go on a date with this guy.

"You have a date," I say firmly. "With me."

Her eyes widen in surprise, and I feel the burst of victory. Aha. Finally rendered her speechless. Heck, I rendered myself speechless.

Hazel turns to me, folding her arms across her chest as

130

Easy as Pie

she glares at me. "You have got to be kidding me. Now you choose to do this? Now?"

She practically rolls her eyes.

"Please excuse him. He's been away from town for too long." She grinds out that last part with a fierce tone. "He forgot about the auction dates for the benefit dinner."

Auction dates?

I stare at the back of her head since she's practically wedged herself between Adam and me.

The man looks back and forth between us, looking utterly confused.

Hazel is glaring at me. That is not a good sign. She takes a step toward me, her boots clicking against the concrete floor of the coffee shop.

"Tripp Sharpe."

I sincerely debate fleeing before she catches me. "Hazel." I hold my hands up in the air.

"Hazel, don't do something that I know you're thinking about doing."

She narrows her eyes at me, "I haven't lost my temper since high school. But I'm willing to break that streak."

The flashing anger in her eyes tells me she's not kidding.

I lean back to watch the man leave the coffee shop. He pauses and lifts his hand in a wave in my direction before he walks out the door. When I turn back to Hazel, she's still glaring daggers at me. "I'm wondering if I need to get out of arm's reach or leave the building entirely."

"You marched into my conversation, took it over, and ruined my chance at possibly having a date with a cute boy."

I rest my elbow on the chair nonchalantly. "A boy, really?

Because I think you should look for a man." My insightful little comment does not go over well with her.

Her eyes widen, her nostrils flare, and I turn around to hurry back to the table. I sit down behind my laptop. I'm careful to keep the table in between us, in case she decides to go all hawkish on me.

"You are in big trouble," she whispers threateningly to me across the table. She plants both her hands on the surface, leaning forward. Blonde hair slips out of her topknot, falling around her face.

"Hazel, why don't you sit down? We'll talk about some benefits—dinner things." I try to distract her with a project. She does not take the bait.

"I'm going out for a walk. I'm going to call Adam and apologize for *your* behavior. Then, I'm going to ignore you."

Something I appreciate about Hazel when she's mad; there's no guessing. You don't have to wonder if she's mad at you; you'll know it. She doesn't mess around with her anger.

Chapter 24

Hazel

I cannot believe Tripp said he had a date with me. Just when I shoved him into the too-small best friend box, he had to pop out like a Jack-in-the-box, scaring the crap right out of me and making my heart pitter-patter dangerously.

I angrily left the coffee shop—and to make matters worse, I forgot my mocha on the counter. Tripp had chased after me with a million apologies, but I shut him down when I climbed into my car and sped away.

When I get back home, I send a text to Aria and Daisy, asking if they want to do a girls' night tonight.

Aria: Yes. Please. I had a child ask if I had grandkids today. Please make me feel 21 again.

Daisy: PLEASE <3

Hazel: Dinner?

Aria: MULLIGAN's

Daisy: All of the above.

By the time I change in my apartment and come downstairs ready to do some angry work, Aria and Daisy have texted back.

Dinner and drinks are confirmed for Mulligan's bar tonight. Thank goodness.

It's time for a distraction. And who knows? Maybe I'll take Floyd up on his advice and find myself a boyfriend. That will take care of any weird outbursts Tripp has.

Oh boy. I forgot how busy Mulligan's can be. Or how loud. But it's the perfect combination for me to forget my anger.

I was busy trying to thank Adam for the recommendation to the *World Mechanic* magazine and then invite him to the benefit dinner. Tripp charged in, thinking I was setting up a date, when really, I was inviting Adam to participate in the date auction.

And why would Tripp say I already had a date? And with him, no less? It makes zero sense. He knows I'm still deciding if I want a date or not. I mean, I could text Hanson, he would be up for it. Or maybe there's someone here.

I scan the busy bar. And I'll take care of that little problem tonight. There has to be at least one desperate, lonely man in this bar who would be willing to be my benefit dinner date.

I check my phone and see if Aria and Daisy are running late, but when I look back up, my eyes land on a couple of familiar heads.

Mia's hair is so dark it practically reflects the lights. And Parker—well, Parker looks deep in conversation with Mia.

I went to high school with both of them, but we didn't

really become friends until this year. They're great because they're busy with work, making them the ultimate low-maintenance friends. The last time I saw them was at this same bar. It's where Mia likes to hang out. Parker is the PR manager for the local minor hockey league. The Appies. She's made them popular on TikTok, which is saying something because I hadn't realized Harvest Hollow *had* a minor league until Parker took over management. She's given me a very strict "No dating hockey players" commandment.

Unfortunately for her, one of her players had come over and introduced himself that night. I never did text him, which is sad, because he gave me his number but didn't take mine. I personally think it's the sweetest gesture when a guy leaves the choice up to you.

And right now, when I need a date the most, I regret not texting him.

Mia spots me and I wave extra big. She points to the empty seat beside her just as Parker turns around and waves at me, too.

I hold up my phone and point at it, as if that will explain that I'm meeting someone else. Mia blows me a kiss.

My phone chimes as I hold it above my head, so I unlock it and read the text, realizing I missed seeing Daisy and Aria in the corner close to the restrooms.

As I make my way across the room, a loud cheer catches my attention.

There's a crowd of men around a table. Some are standing, and some sit relaxed in chairs. It's several of the hockey players, a few of whom are still wearing some Appie apparel.

I bump into an empty chair just as I catch a blonde hockey player's eye. *It's the one who gave me his number.*

I freeze briefly because he really *is* that good-looking.

He grins at me and tips his beer toward me.

I smile back and give him a jaunty salute, then tip my head toward the girls' table.

He winks and turns back to the guys, and I hurry to the table.

"What's wrong?" Aria demands as I sit down. She pushes an old-fashioned toward me.

"Why would you ask that?" I ask.

Daisy points at the glass. "Because you drank that like a shot."

Wow. It's empty already. Who did that?

"Tripp is being weird." I clear my throat. "No, I'm being weird."

They look at me sympathetically.

"So, when did you wake up and realize Tripp is a gorgeous-looking man with a personality you could happily spend the rest of your life with?" Daisy asks as she plants her chin in her hands.

I scowl as I look at her. "You haven't even met him yet!"

"I know. But I've heard enough about him. And I've seen him from a distance."

Aria looks at me, her brown eyes watching every movement I make. "Quit it. You're acting like you can read my mind."

"Maybe I can," she teases.

"I'll take finding a creepy exorcist for three hundred, please." I practically roll my eyes. Whatever Aria is thinking it's probably wrong. I'm sure of it.

"So, what's the trouble with Tripp?" Aria asks seriously.

"He's gatekeeping my dates. Like he's gone all overprotective brother on me," I say as I spin the glass slowly on the table.

Aria looks disappointed. "Dang, I was hoping he was getting jealous of you."

See? She was thinking the wrong thing.

And it does nothing to help having her voice that idea. "No, I need him to step away from the big brother routine. I'd like to have a date someday."

"Don't look now, but there's a gorgeous man making his way over here," Daisy whispers—which is really not a whisper. It's more of a yell. "Do we know him?"

And, because I have zero self-control, I turn to look. Blondie is making his way over to us.

I smile and wave when he hesitates. Bless his heart, he actually makes sure women are interested in him, too.

"Hi," he says as I slide over a chair and make room for him to sit down beside me.

"Helloooo." I drag out with a smile.

"I was hoping to see you again," he says as he plants both elbows on the table. "But you haven't introduced me to your friends yet."

And kind to the people around him. He's definitely a keeper. "It depends...are you the kind of guy a person introduces to their friends?" I tease.

He smiles at Aria and Daisy. "Definitely."

Aria and Daisy have no problem introducing themselves and Eli takes a long time shaking each of their hands.

He turns back to me. "Drinks at Mulligan's again? I'm beginning to think you're a creature of habit."

"Only where a good old-fashioned is concerned." I point to the empty glass.

"I'll get you another," he suggests.

"I'll take you up on it...if I can ask you something."

Eli runs a hand down his face, pretending to change it to a serious look. "Anything for you."

"Better be careful with that line. Someday a woman will take you up on that," Daisy pipes up, and Eli chuckles.

"Have you heard of the Harvest Hollow Benefit Dinner?"

"Yes, a little bit. I think Mia mentioned something about it after I met you."

I swallow the lump in my throat as I realize he'd been asking about me.

Someone from the hockey table yells Eli's name, and he waves them off.

"I'm needing someone to be my wingman," I say slowly. I've never asked someone out on a date before. It's more natural for me to ask him as a friend. It's the only way I can get the words out so I'll approach it like that...

"You mean a date," he asks, calling my bluff. So much for playing it smooth.

"Yes, a date, but I didn't want to pressure you," I say with a grin.

"Please pressure me. I'll suffer through your company if I have to."

"It might be kind of boring because my main job is to walk around and make sure everything is going smoothly. But I'd love to spend the evening with someone fun."

"I promise to distract you from all the boring parts," he says as he crosses his heart.

"You're a great sport. I'll bribe you with good food and drinks," I promise.

He winks. "And don't forget good company."

Someone yells his name again.

"I'm about to get in trouble if I don't get back there. It's supposed to be guys night only. But text me the details, and I'll wear an outfit that matches your eyes."

With that, he returns to his friends across the bar. We watch as he gets jostled back and forth.

"If things don't work out there..." Aria says as she waggles her eyebrows.

"You have a date! And you didn't get blocked by Tripp!" Daisy says with a smile.

She's right.

I have a date, and Tripp wasn't here to do anything about it. Success feels good.

Chapter 25

Hazel

Waking up after a night at Mulligan's is not as easy as it was five years ago. But I have to repair a drive shaft and have two other tune-ups that are getting dropped off after lunch.

When I walk down my stairs wearing my coveralls, ready to blast some music and work, Tripp is parked in my driveway.

I guess he's serious about this apology because he should know better than to be here so soon when I'm still furious. How dare he make me feel things and then shut me down?

That weird overprotective brother moment could have been misconstrued as jealousy by a delusional soul. *By my delusional soul*, to be exact.

I ignore Tripp and unlock the main door. I flip the lights on and turn on the space heater, letting it warm up the area while I slip my tennis shoes off and grab my work boots out of the basket in the corner. I learned a long time ago that bringing greasy boots into a home was a recipe for stained furniture. Grease seemed to have its own travel plan. It never stayed on the front rug. So now I keep the boots here in the shop and the only time I wear coveralls in the house is if they're fresh out of the washer.

My brilliant ignore-Tripp-plan is foiled when he follows me into the shop.

I roll my tool chest over to the car, where I'm replacing the timing belt.

"What can I do to help you?" Tripp asks.

I grimace as I try to smile at him.

"Oh, I think I've got everything handled." I stretch my lips a little wider, hoping that it's a convincing smile. Not because I don't appreciate his olive branch, but because Tripp is anything but mechanically minded. It's not his game.

He smirks. "You think I'm going to break something, don't you?"

This time my smile is genuine. "I never said that."

"You didn't have to. I can read your mind. Don't you know?" he teases.

"You're incorrigible," I tell him with a laugh.

"Okay, fine, I won't do anything that will break the car. But at least I can sit here and hand you tools."

"Shouldn't you be catching up on some sleep or something like that right now?"

"No, I'm still in the best friend doghouse for being weird. I'm here to make things less weird."

"You realize by saying 'weird' so many times, you've *definitely* made it weird now." I raise my eyebrows at him.

He throws back his head and laughs. "I'll see if I can work that word in every conversation today."

"Who says I'm talking to you yet?" I ask with raised eyebrows.

"I thought you might be able to forgive me since I'm an idiot, and I brought you apple cider donuts from Cataloochee."

I glance at the box he's pointing to. There's a coffee cup beside it.

Brushing my hands against my coveralls, I walk over to the shelf the box is sitting on. I take a long sip of the salted caramel mocha, then grab a donut from the box and eat it in two bites.

"You're forgiven."

He has a gleeful smile and his face and looks so pleased with himself. "Now can I help?"

I unlock the tool chest and flip open the lid. "Okay, you can hand me stuff. I need to have this car done by noon. Would be nice to not have to be grabbing stuff out all the time."

Tripp grabs the bar stool I have floating around the shop and wheels it over next to the tool chest. "I'll be your surgeon's assistant today."

"Okay, could you hand me the Pac-Man?"

He hesitates a minute, then nods. "Of course, I can hand you that. Or him."

I smirk at him. He doesn't know what I'm talking about.

I turn to go grab it myself, but he waves me away.

"Absolutely not. No, no, I will figure this out. Tell me what it looks like." He holds up a hand. "Actually, don't. I just googled it, and I think I know."

"I don't know if this is going to make my job go any faster."

"Aha! Gotcha!" he exclaims as he turns to look at the drawer; eventually, I'm pretty sure he'll organize everything.

"Want me to organize while I'm looking?" the mind reader teases. He knows I have a method for my non-organization. He's so proud of having found the Pac-Man, that I don't say anything and try not to cringe. Then he slams the drawer.

His face goes blank. His eyes glaze over. The Pac-Man drops to the floor.

There's a very soft gasp that escapes his lips. I look down at his hand, which is now partially trapped in the heavy drawer. It looks like it's the side of his hand by his thumb.

I stare. Those drawers close tight. They're designed to keep out any possible water damage, and *his hand is trapped in there.*

"Hazel, I think the door locked. We need the key." His voice is strained as he tries to pull the drawer open again, and I jump into action.

Unfortunately, it jars his hand every time I try to unlock it. He gives a very quiet moan.

"I'm sorry. I'm sorry, I'm sorry. I'm sorry. I'm sorry." My chanting isn't helping anyone.

Finally, the drawer unlocks, and I pull it open with a jerk. This time there's a quiet sound coming from that strained face. His jaw is clenched tight, and his eyes squint as he tries to pull in a long breath.

"I shouldn't have opened the drawer so fast. I should have known it would hurt. Does it hurt?" I stare at his face, scared to look down at his hand.

He nods grimly. He's not afraid to look at his own hand and takes a moment to assess the damage.

"Hazel. Ha ha." That 'ha ha' does not sound promising.

"Hazel," he starts again. "Don't look."

Do you know all those times when you know someone's telling you something for a reason, and it's a good reason, but you decide to ignore them?

Well, I ignore him and look at the hand.

It's bad. *Real* bad. There's a cut along the edge of his hand, and blood is running—rolling—dripping—

I gag. I squeeze my eyes shut, but all I see is that deep red.

I wobble, and I feel Tripp grab my arm to steady me. "Hazel!"

The next thing I know, I open my eyes to stare into Tripp's face. It's pale, and he's scowling.

I'm also laid across his lap like a cat and he has some disposable shop towels wrapped around his cut hand. He's sitting on the ground, resting his back against the offending tool chest.

I'm not sure how we got down here so fast.

"I'm sorry."

I scramble to push off his lap.

"You almost hit your head," he says. Funny how he sounds more worried about me when he's the one who's bleeding.

I look at his hand. The blood is starting to soak through.

"Get in the car now. You need a doctor." I pop up. Soaking blood is fine. Running blood is not. And I will think about happy things.

The time Tripp baked a pie, and it tasted terrible because he thought it needed three times the salt.

That time we ate an entire carton of chocolate chip ice cream because we both failed a chemistry test.

The time we decided to join choir. Neither of us can carry a tune in a bucket.

I grab more shop towels and wrap his hand three more times. His face is pale, and he's lost the ability to force a smile even.

I don't have time to think about flowing blood.

"Get in the car." I hold his wrist and help him to his feet. I hurry him out the shop door and toward his own car out front. Mine's still parked in the garage in the back. "Where are your keys?"

"Back pocket," he says quietly.

Any other day, I would be marveling that I get to touch Tripp's butt as I slip my hand into his back left pocket.

Today I'm trying to make sure he doesn't bleed out and that I don't pass out and kill us both as we drive to the hospital.

He's able to climb into the passenger seat all by himself, which is great because I have to focus on getting this electric car started. I don't get the opportunity to drive them often.

After a few wrong buttons, I managed to get us on the road and speeding toward the hospital.

I pass the garbage truck on a blind corner and earn a long honk from an oncoming sedan. "How are you holding up?" I ask grimly as I dodge past a mailman.

It's quiet for a minute, and in a panic, I turn to look at him.

He's not passed out and slumped against the window. Instead, he's calmly staring at me with a contemplative look on his face.

"You're taking care of me. Blood and all."

"Tripp. Please don't say blood at a time like this, or I might not be able to take care of you." I suck in a breath of clean car air. A soft vanilla air freshener can do wonders for a car. Slamming on my brakes, I turn onto a side street to avoid getting stuck behind a school bus.

"You're a hell of a best friend, Hazel. I don't know what I would do without you."

"Well if I don't get you to the ER soon, then I'm going to be writing your funeral speech. But I'll make sure it's a good one." I screech into the hospital parking lot like I've got all the traffic rights of an ambulance.

This elicits a rough chuckle from him. "It's not that bad, Hazel, I promise. It only hurts. Makes me a little lightheaded."

Luckily there's a parking space open in the back of the building, and since Tripp has the hospital pass, we're able to park there. I rush around to his side and open the door.

Reaching for his good arm, I pull him out to stand and loop my arm around his waist.

"My legs aren't broken," he teases quietly as we start for the hospital doors.

"I'm going to catch you if you pass out," I promise. Because how on earth someone can look at that much blood and not pass out is beyond me.

Blood is meant to be on the inside—not the outside.

I will firmly stand by that statement.

The receptionist takes one look at who's standing in front of her and points to the triage station around the corner. We walk in and are greeted instantly.

"What did the cat drag in?" The triage nurse—Patty her

name tag says—is gaping at the two of us. Bless her heart, she stops teasing when she spies the now blood-soaked disposable towels. "Oh, dear."

"I saved a small child from an avalanche," Tripp teases her. She slowly unwraps it, and I have to stare at that speckled ceiling.

"Hmmm, somehow I don't think that's what happened," she mutters.

Wow, they need a new cleaning crew. There are cobwebs around the ceiling sprinklers.

"I'm going to prep another room because you're going to need stitches."

"If I could have glued it, I would have," Tripp replies with a laugh.

Patty shakes her head. "I'll be right back."

"Hazel, it's okay if you want to wait in the waiting room," Tripp says with a grim look on his face. "You're not going to want to see this part."

Okay, well, that was a little bit blunt and probably true, but the way his pale face is looking at me right now, it's not like I can just go sit down and leave him to bleed out in a stranger's arms. Doesn't matter that he actually works with this woman and that she seems very competent, I know, though, that if I were to be the one hurt, Tripp wouldn't leave my side.

I take a deep breath of sterile hospital air and smile at him. "I've always wanted to learn how to sew. Let's go."

He focuses on me, and his eyes warm. "Thanks, Hazel."

"Oh this? Easy as pie."

He leans over and whispers, "You mean as easy as baking a pie on a rollercoaster?"

"Precisely. Don't push your luck, Sharpe."

Patty comes back to bring us to the prepped room. We follow her into an enclosed room similar to a regular doctor's office. Not exactly the surgery space I was imagining. Don't they pull out all the red tape for an injury like this? This seems a little casual to me.

We're greeted by a doctor in her early thirties. Chestnut-colored hair and brown skin. She smiles at Tripp. "Funny seeing you here again."

"Dr. Banik. Good to see you again."

"Should we put this on the loudspeaker? Because I'm pretty sure everyone is going to want to know how this happened. And Patty's probably already spreading the news." Her smile is pretty much diabolical, which makes me like her immediately.

But I also take pity on Tripp because it's pretty much my fault that he's here. I should have warned him that the drawers shut fast.

"He was helping me at work and shut his hand in a drawer," I throw out there.

The doctor finally turns to me. "Tripp, I didn't know you were married. I'm Veda Banik."

Oh, I definitely like her. I smile. "Tripp's my best friend."

"My husband is my best friend too. It's the best foundation for marriage," she nods as though we're on the same page. We're not even in the same book.

"We're not married," Tripp interjects.

Dr. Banik nods again as she washes her hands in the sink and then gloves up. "Better get a ring on it soon. She might figure out there are men out there that don't shut their hands in drawers."

I *like* this woman.

She proceeds to examine Tripp's injury and since I can't bear to look, I reach over and latch onto his good hand.

"Feel free to squeeze my hand," I offer as I stare at the wall.

The squeeze doesn't come, just a calloused thumb stroking the back of my hand. "Thanks, Hazel."

"I won't tell anyone if you scream," I promise him. "And Dr. Banik is sworn by the Hippocratic Oath. So, your secret's safe."

His hand squeezes mine lightly. "How about you tell me who you have lined up for dates?"

"Dates?" Dr. Banik pipes up.

"We have a benefit dinner at the end of the month. I can get you the information for it if you're interested. It's a fundraiser for ovarian cancer." I pause, not sure how much information I should spill right now, especially since I'm nervous as it is.

"I would love to look at the information," she says kindly. Her voice is muffled as if she's turned her back to me or is bent over Tripp's other hand. She's not speaking to him at all, because she doesn't need to. He knows the exact process for stitching up a hand. He probably would have done it himself, except he injured his dominant hand.

"We're doing a date night auction. But I'm trying to figure out the actual logistics of it and how to keep it fun—without too much awkwardness. Obviously, it's going to be a little awkward, but that's the fun part. I'm thinking of having them sit at a banquet table with papers in front for a silent auction-type thing. I'll put it next to the coffee bar. That way, there's lots of traffic right there, and people won't feel weird."

"It sounds great, Hazel," Tripp says just before he grunts. Oh no. I don't want to think about why he's grunting.

"And then we could have a specific date already planned. I don't want anyone feeling the pressure to plan something, and since we're the ones planning the fundraiser and they're just helping, I'll give everyone gift cards to a specific local restaurant where they'll take their date buyer to dinner."

I gasp. "Am I the one getting my hand stitched? Because I'm pretty sure I'm rambling as though I am."

Tripp and Dr. Banik laugh. "You're doing great," Tripp assures me.

Dr. Banik jumps in to encourage me, "It's so much better to have a rambler than a screamer or a worrier, don't you think?"

Tripp replies, "I completely agree. Rambling is nice. Makes everything go faster, and everyone is calmer. You're a natural at this, Hazel."

"Don't get used to it. Next time I expect you to keep your hand out of the drawer before you close it. It shouldn't be that hard to do."

Tripp chuckles and squeezes my hand again. "I'll do my best...but no promises."

Chapter 26

Hazel

Tripp: I'm having trouble buttoning my pants.

Hazel: Put on sweatpants.

Tripp: Please help.

Hazel: No.

Waking up to Tripp texting me about his wardrobe malfunctions would have normally made me laugh, but I really do feel bad about the whole drawer incident. He was busy trying to make up for being weird, and then I forgot to warn him about the drawer. It's pretty much my fault he's having trouble putting pants on with stitches in his hand.

Tripp: I have the next two days off to let my hand recover. Want to do something?

And that's how I ended up driving to his apartment and parking on the street below his window. The building has locked access, so I text him to let him know I'm here.

The door flies open with a bang, and Tripp walks out wearing gray sweatpants and black tennis shoes. He holds up his hand like a trophy. "You didn't help."

"I'm here now, aren't I?" I laugh. "Besides, I'm not putting your pants on."

He lifts his eyebrows and asks, "Does that mean you'll help me take them off?"

I decide to ignore *that* loaded question and ask, "What did you have in mind?"

"If we don't get apple cider at Harvest Farms, what are we even doing with our lives?" He shrugs as if it's the most obvious choice to go spend our day at the local produce farm. He's actually not too far off the mark since I need to check in on the donation Dad has already arranged with Bill and Patty Ethans, the Harvest Farms owners.

"I couldn't agree more. Get in. We'll mix business with pleasure."

Tripp looks at my car parked behind his on the street. He slowly turns to stare at me. "I'd like to be able to keep the cider in my stomach if it's okay with you."

"You don't think I've matured in my driving?"

"No. I rode with you to the hospital. I remembered exactly why I prefer to drive."

"You were in danger!"

"Yes, I definitely was, and it wasn't from that little cut on my hand." He takes a step forward toward me, a gloating look on his face.

I plant my fists on my hips and smile threateningly back at him, taking a step forward. "I'm a very responsible, conscientious driver."

He takes another step forward into my personal space bubble, but I refuse to back down. I step forward a couple more inches and my chest brushes against his. Those gray sweatpants are soft against the back of my hands.

His eyes widen, then that smirk turns positively evil.

"First one to the driver's seat?"

I smile back. "It's a deal."

It's the first time in my life that overalls betray me.

As I turn to run for the car, Tripp latches on to the back of my overalls and steers me around to face the building while he nonchalantly sits down in the driver's seat.

I'm choking on air. Or despair. Not sure which at this rate.

He lets go of the straps after he starts the car. Because, yes, I left my keys sitting right there. "Get in and buckle up, buttercup. We have a pumpkin patch to go to!"

I point at him threateningly and he grins, those dimples taunting me.

"You have an injured hand. You shouldn't be driving!"

"Look, I'll take my chances at a slow, steady pace."

I look at him and whisper, "Coward."

He throws up his wrapped hand and wiggles it. "What are you going to do about it? Pull an injured man from a vehicle?"

I fold my arms across my chest. "I'm thinking about it, honestly."

"Aw, come on. We need to go to the pumpkin patch."

I sigh. "Right. Tickets. Fundraisers. All the things."

Tripp looks at me. "No, we need to go drink hot apple cider and have fun."

I trudge around to the passenger side and climb in while he pulls out and begins weaving his way through the busy downtown traffic.

Tripp's phone rings, and he answers it after a few

fumbled attempts with his bandaged hand. He hits the speakerphone button and sets it on the dash. "Hello?"

"Hey, so Meyer wants to know about this best friend of yours. Is she—"

"In the car with me? Yes, she is." Tripp looks embarrassed as he tries to turn down the volume. His attempts have him almost swerving and he gives up. As if that will magically make me unhear what he said.

"Hazel? Hazel, are you there?" an unfamiliar male voice asks me.

"It depends on who's asking!" I reply with a laugh.

"Hi, this is Archie, Tripp's number-one best friend."

Tripp chuckles at that and pushes his baseball cap to rest tilted up. "Ignore him. He's just upset that I gave the top spot to you."

"I'm a poor loser," Archie admits. "Meyer wants to know when you both are coming to visit."

"Wait, is this your Oregon friend?" I ask, sincerely enjoying myself now.

"It's not Orrr-eeeee-goooone. It's Oirgun," Archie declares.

"I can tell you're a little touchy about the being number two thing..." I tease.

Tripp turns to grin at me as he turns onto the country road that leads to Harvest Farms.

"We're going to have the Best Friend Games when you come to visit. A rigorous competition of hiking, bocce ball, kayaking, and feeding friends."

"Turns out I make a mean pumpkin bread, but I hate hiking. I've kayaked once, and I've never played bocce ball."

"It sounds like it's not going to end very well for you then, doesn't it?" Archie sounds so smug.

Another voice pipes up, "You flipped your kayak in the first fifteen seconds yesterday—and not on purpose."

Tripp looks like he's about to have tears running down his cheeks from laughing so hard. Somehow, he manages to maneuver the car into Harvest Farms parking lot, dodging a twelve-passenger van pulling out.

"That's Meyer yelling in the background," Tripp explains when he catches his breath.

"Listen Archie, you name the time and the place, and I'll remind you why you're number two."

There's an evil chuckle and Meyer's voice saying, "Archie, you're outmatched."

"It's on. Okay. Excuse me, I have to hang up and go practice my rowing," Archie says.

The call disconnects, and I turn to stare at Tripp. "No wonder you enjoyed the West Coast if you're hanging out with people like that. They sound fun." I hold up a hand. "Minus the whole hiking bit."

Tripp shuts off the car and climbs out. I grab my sweatshirt and tug the hood up to block the crisp wind, then step out.

"So, what's bocce ball?"

"I'd be happy to teach you," he says as he locks the car. Then holds up his injured hand. "When this heals, that is. Now, let's go find that apple cider."

We make our way to the small coffee shop-style shed where they're selling apple cider and pumpkin spice lattes. This is a farm experience I can get behind.

Little families milling about. Preschools out on field

trips. It's not just a small pumpkin patch in someone's back yard. Harvest Farms has become an entire experience. People drive from an hour away just to spend the day here.

With hayrides, haunted corn mazes, apple guns, and—

"MEHHHH." A loud shriek has me jumping forward and grasping Tripp's arm.

"What the heck was that?" I ask as I look around. Ah, yes, how could I forget the Harvest Farms petting zoo?

Tripp points to a pen across the driveway. There are straw bales sitting inside the wooden panels and a small goat staring directly at us.

"MEHHHH."

"Do you suppose it's demon-possessed?" I whisper.

Another goat runs up to chase off the screamer, and they begin to play tag around the pen.

I glance up to find Tripp's amused stare fixed on my face. "All these years, and I didn't know you were scared of goats."

"I'm not scared of *all* goats, but I'm pretty sure that one was staring into my soul." I check over my shoulder one more time before I tighten the strings on my sweatshirt hood.

Tripp reaches forward and tugs them tighter with his uninjured hand. "So, are we here for business or pleasure?"

I stop and stare at him. "Definitely pleasure. Then business."

"Lead the way, Hazelnut. I'll follow you anywhere."

Oh Trippy. If only you knew what those words do to me.

"That pumpkin is as big as a VW Bug," Tripp says as he stares at a giant pumpkin at the entrance of the pumpkin field. We satisfied our hot apple cider craving and spoke with Bill and Patty Ethans, and now we're on a mission to find the perfect decorative pumpkin for my dad's porch.

"There's no way that thing is real," I say.

He picks his way forward over pumpkin vines and knocks on it. "It sounds like a pumpkin, at least. Can you imagine trying to haul this one home to decorate your yard?"

We both laugh. It's all the way up to Tripp's shoulder. This thing is breaking records somewhere, I'm sure of it.

"You'd need a tow truck to move it," Tripp snorts.

We move out of the way so a small family can take their family photo in front of it.

"Are we going to go check out the venue tomorrow after my shift?" Tripp asks as we walk through the pumpkin field.

"I can't tomorrow," I say as I pick up the cutest little pumpkin. It's like the baby of a baby pumpkin, and it will be lonely if I don't buy it and bring it home.

"Hazel, it'll be Saturday."

"Yes, and the next day after that is Sunday."

He snorts. "Thank you, Hazelnut. But what I meant was that hopefully you're not working that much, are you? Are you working seven days a week?"

"No, but I have something going on tomorrow."

He looks at me suspiciously. "How about tomorrow late afternoon after you do whatever it is you're doing?"

"Well, I'm not sure how long they'll stay—" I cut myself off.

Tripp laughs as he steps over a lopsided pumpkin.

"You're being incredibly vague. And now you have me really curious...do you have a date you're not telling me about?"

I might imagine it, but it looks like he might be frowning.

"Please, that went so well last time you got nosy about my possible dates." I point at his hand. "Why are you so overprotective now?"

Now he's definitely frowning, but he doesn't say anything.

We stumble over pumpkin vines, and I regret wearing my tennis shoes out to the muddy patch. The floral pattern on these ones is taking on some very brown colors.

"You're not going to tell me what's happening? Curiosity is going to kill me. Tomorrow I'll be sitting there on that uncomfortable couch in my apartment, wondering what you're up to."

"Read a book. It'll keep you busy."

"I'm so tired of reading medical textbooks," he sighs as if that's the *only* genre of books in the world.

"Then go read a mystery. Or a romance. I don't care. Do something with your life while I'm busy." I toss a smile over my shoulder so he knows I'm teasing, but he's not actually looking at me. He's busy picking a tall, skinny pumpkin.

"I haven't read a fiction book outside of what was assigned in school," he says with a grunt.

"You're joking. I thought you were being dramatic when we were at the bookstore."

"It's not fun for me to sit down and read a book." He hoists the pumpkin and carries it under one arm like it's no big deal. "So, if you don't tell me what you're up to, I'll have to make my own assumptions."

He looks at me out of the corner of his eye, leaving a nice empty threat hanging there...

"I'm doing a magazine shoot," I whisper, caving to the peer pressure.

His head snaps up at this. "You're what?"

I don't say anything more at this point because I know he heard me.

"What magazine?"

"*World Mechanic*." I look up to see him smiling at me.

"Hazel Preston, are you embarrassed?" There's a grin on his face, and if I were a violent person, I would think about leaning forward and smacking it off. With this tiny little pumpkin. Good thing I'm not.

Instead, I nod slowly, and watch in confusion as Tripp sets down his pumpkin, and then leaps forward to scoop me into his arms. In fact, he wraps one arm around me and lifts me off the ground, while keeping his injured hand away. I'm pressed against his hard chest and it feels nice. "You're going to be in a magazine!!"

He spins me around, and I have to cling to him to keep from accidentally kicking any innocent passersby.

"You're going to be in a magazine!" he repeats as he slides me back down to the ground, and I have the privilege of feeling every hard muscle on my way back to the dirt.

"It sounds like it's 1999," I joke, as I'm all too aware that he hasn't let go of me yet.

"Hey, it's not just a magazine—*World Mechanic* still has a good online presence. This is great! I'm shocked you're actually doing it!"

"Me too. But I don't know, it feels right. And actually, the guys helped talk me into it."

"Ahh, the infamous morning mechanics. They're some good guys."

Floyd, Henry, and Jean. I wouldn't be half the mechanic I am without them. They've been steady supporters of me since I picked up my first socket wrench. They've taught me lots of tips and tricks that no book or class ever has.

And Tripp? He's always believed I can do anything I set my mind to, and it seems like that hasn't changed.

"Yeah, if you must know, the guy I was talking to at the coffee shop was the one who recommended me to them. I was wondering why he was being so friendly, but I guess it was because of the magazine."

A quick frown flashes across Tripp's face. "You're going to do amazing. But if anything about it makes you feel awkward, call me, and I'll be there right away."

Chapter 27

Hazel

World *Mechanic* is showing up at my door today. Dad and Milo helped clean the shop yesterday afternoon; Adam Reeves texted and said he would be meeting me here too, and I'm pretty sure I'm sweating through an entire tube of deodorant.

An interview with a magazine? What was I thinking? I don't even have an official name for my shop. Hazel's Hot Wheels is a joke. What would a serious mechanic name her shop?

Instead of wearing my typical fall coveralls, I throw on the overalls that I usually wear in the summer heat. Not as hot, but still, plenty of pockets for stashing tools or nuts and bolts. Plus, I don't have any clean coveralls for this. And while I'm not embarrassed to be seen covered in grease, I am doing a shop photo shoot, and I'd like to look semi-decent.

I want them to know that I can be feminine and be a mechanic. Just like my mom taught me. I don't have to pick one or the other. I can replace carburetors with painted nails. With that in mind, I slip on one of my favorite pairs of floral tennis shoes. Not the ones I wore to the pumpkin patch. These ones don't have mud on them.

There are three people standing in my driveway when I come outside.

Adam and a woman with dark hair that actually looks good in a low pony, and not like a young Colonial man. There's another man who looks in his mid-thirties with a camera bag in his hands.

"Hazel, hey, sorry we're early!" Adam calls out with a smile.

"No problem. I'm sorry I didn't realize you were here yet; I would have hurried out."

"No problem," the woman says as she sweeps the long pony over her shoulder. *Deep hair envy here.* She extends her hand. "I'm Madge Cohen."

"Hazel Preston." I reach out and shake her hand.

"I'm the director for the *World Mechanic* website and magazine," she says, as though we haven't corresponded over email or text the last couple weeks.

I smile brightly at her. "It's really great to meet you. I've followed that site for a while now and really enjoy what you have to offer."

"That's great to hear. When Adam called me and said he had someone new for me to interview, I was excited to come out and meet you. And see something new."

There's an awkward silence as she glances around the property. A cute, but small craftsman house. A shop that's large enough to work in but might not seem up to big city standards...the silence is killing me, so I ask, "Are you based on the West Coast?"

"Nevada. Adam used to work with us before he decided to desert us for the Harvest Hollow." She glances at him over her shoulder. It's a teasing yet loaded remark which Adam shrugs off.

"It was time for something new," he says, by way of explanation.

"Anyway, I'm glad he called, because as you can imagine, we don't have a lot of interviewees that are women."

"Which is a real shame," I throw out immediately.

She nods and continues, "Anyway, I would love to write a feature piece on you if you would like that. A picture of you on the front of the magazine? Something sexy but also functional?"

"I'm not sure I can deliver both those at the same time," I reply dryly.

Adam catches my eye and gives me a conspiratorial wink.

Madge looks around. "I'm going to look at settings and see what we have to work with on the photo front."

She snaps her fingers—yes, snaps them like she's at a poetry reading—and walks toward the shop with the other man in tow.

"I'm not sure if I should thank you or do something else entirely," I admit to Adam.

He shrugs. "Madge can be a bit over the top. And sometimes blunt, but she'll definitely shine a light on your business. You'll have more people phoning you to fix your car than you can handle. She's good at getting eyes on businesses. We call her the blog doc. She can salvage any dying business and make a go of it."

I look at him flatly. "If she wants me to look sexy, I flat-out refuse."

"You already look great to me."

"I swear if it ends up only being my butt on the cover of that magazine, I'm blaming you."

"And I will accept full responsibility because I made it clear to Madge that you're not playing mechanic, this is your job."

Turns out my fears about Madge were unfounded. She asked specific questions that led me to talk about my work: the thing I was most comfortable with.

I explained to her about my last project of rebuilding a carburetor, and she seemed genuinely interested in it. I was *not* as impressed with the photographer, who kept suggesting maybe I unbuckle those overalls.

Finally, they decide they wanted a few shots of me standing in front of the open bay into the shop, so I open the large rolling door, and Madge and the photographer go outside to determine the best lighting while Adam walks over to stand next to me.

"So, what exactly was your role at *World Mechanic*?" I ask Adam as we watch Madge and the photographer move back and forth across the driveway.

He shoves his hands in his pockets and looks around. "It wasn't a large role—"

Madge cuts him off. "He didn't tell you? How like him. Adam *owns World Mechanic* website and magazine."

I narrow my eyes, then mouth a few choice words.

Luckily, she's called away by the man with the camera—I still can't remember his name.

"Wowwww." I drag out the word as I turn to look at Adam skeptically.

He shakes his head, guilt plastered across his face. "It

wasn't fair of me to surprise you like that. I honestly wanted to give you business."

I study him. "No ulterior motives?"

"None. Besides, your boyfriend would have a few choice words to say to me if I did." He laughs.

I don't have to guess who he's talking about. "Oh, Tripp isn't my boyfriend."

He nods. "Keep telling yourself that, and maybe someday the world will believe it, too."

I plant both hands on my hips as I face him completely. "What's that supposed to mean?"

He sighs. "Well, maybe *you* honestly believe that, but I can say Tripp doesn't."

"What makes you say that?"

"He jumped down my throat at the coffee shop when he thought I was trying to take you out on a date," Adam reminds me dryly. "So, I promise you don't have anything to worry about. I have something against overprotective-almost-boyfriends, and I don't mess around there."

"I think you're imagining things, but thank you for not having ulterior motives here."

"Aha, but I do have ulterior motives. I need a local to help me get settled. Maybe introduce me to someone who doesn't have a boyfriend—ahem—best friend," he amends when he catches my glare at him.

I laugh. "All right. Well, if you're still game for being a date at the benefit dinner, I'll introduce you to Aria and Daisy."

"Now that sounds great. Okay, Madge is planning to run the article this weekend, I'm pretty sure. So be prepared to get some phone calls and job offers from all fifty states."

"Ha. Now that seems unlikely, but it was still fun to do. Thank you for that. It reminded me that I am getting to do what I love."

Too bad I didn't get to travel or see somewhere new like I'd like to. But maybe that will come someday too.

"Well, how did it go?" Dad asks when I walk inside his house.

"I have no idea. I looked like a fraud, probably."

Dad chuckles. "No, I'm sure you looked like a celebrity."

I sink down into the comfy couch that lines the bay window wall. It's got a butt imprint from me sitting in the same spot over all these years.

I look at Dad. "I don't know if I'm the magazine shoot kind of person."

He smiles at me over the top of his glasses. "You're the kind of person that can be whatever you want to be. It's not many people that are just as comfortable working in a mechanic shop as they are donning formalwear. Just asked me how I know."

That brings a smile to my face. My mom and dad started out as a summer fling. Dad had gone to the Hamptons with some buddies that he knew from the travel baseball league. Summer in the Hamptons was not the norm for Dad. He had been interested in fixing cars from a young age and had already started to take college classes.

But he met my mom that summer. She was the one who grew up in the Hamptons and spent summers on her grandpa's private yacht. They came from two different worlds. But she loved my dad so much that she up and moved to Harvest Hollow to be with him.

She still loved dressing up, and all things party-wise. That's why Dad started the black-tie banquet for her after she passed. Something to honor her memory, something that she would have loved.

Mom loved doing formal holidays. She's the one who passed on a love for doing our makeup and wearing nice dresses. Good clothes. From what I could tell growing up, she never resented Dad for staying in Harvest Hollow, North Carolina. In fact, she loved it. She said that she made her first real friend here. And hoped that Kara and I would get to experience something similar.

"So, what did you think of the magazine shoot?" Dad asks. "Are you ready to be a model?"

"Absolutely not. The photographer wanted me to do a sexy photo shoot. I told him that if they couldn't sell a magazine with a woman mechanic keeping her clothes on, then their company wasn't about mechanic work."

Dad throws back his head and laughs. "What'd they say to that?"

"The owner of the magazine agreed completely with me. The photographer was offended. Apparently, shirtless women are still selling magazines these days. I thought we'd be past this by now, but we're not. It's still a novelty that someone with breasts can work on a car."

Dad snorts. "Ignore those people. Hazel." He pointed at me. "I don't know anyone who can replace a clutch faster than you."

The biggest compliment I can get from Dad. *Also not true.* Dad compliments me all the time. There couldn't be a more supportive dad in the world, which is why it's time for me to bring up the conversation I've avoided.

"Dad, I, uh..." I stare at the ceiling, waiting for it to give me the perfect words to say. The words that have been burning inside my chest for five years.

I swallow the lump in my throat and try again. "Dad."

"I think you've covered that already," Dad teases softly.

I cough into my elbow. "Adam said something about me possibly getting job offers from around the country."

Dad clears his throat twice. "And which state would you pick?"

"Colorado." The word slips out so quickly, I'm surprised. I glance at dad to see how he responds. He was so sneakily smooth in asking that I didn't hesitate to answer, but now that it's out there, I feel bad.

He has his chin resting on his hand while he relaxes in his big chair. That flannel shirt buttoned halfway up over his T-shirt. A cup of coffee that's probably cold by now sitting next to him.

He raises his eyebrows. "Colorado seems a little surprising given how much you hate hiking..."

"Snowboarding. I'd love to go snowboarding there. The ski lift will save me from having to hike. And it would be a short-term thing."

How are we nonchalantly talking about the potential for me to move to Colorado? For a nonexistent job offer. Heck, the article hasn't even been written yet. Adam was probably being an optimist, saying that I would get tons of job offers. A very sweet, delusional optimist.

"Do you want to go?"

"I don't want to leave you," I whisper as I look around the

living room. "But I'd like to see some of the world. Even for a little while."

Mom and Dad's wedding picture hangs above the mantel right next to the crack in the wall. The same crack from when Mom accidentally threw the Wii remote during bowling.

"I think it's time we *both* did something, don't you?" Dad asks.

I stare at him. There's no betrayal, no guilt leaking out of his face at me. No weeping and wailing that I'm leaving him.

To be fair, if he was emotionally manipulative, I'd have an easier time leaving. Instead, he has to be the World's Best Dad. That makes leaving ten times harder.

"I'm considering retiring and maybe doing a little fishing." Dad smiles at me. "Maybe I'll only run the tow truck during busy seasons."

There are lots more calls for the tow truck on holiday weekends...that business model might actually work for him.

"I should have said something sooner. I just didn't realize you felt this way, too, Hazel."

"I didn't want to leave *you*," I admit. "Or have you feel like I'm abandoning the business."

"And I didn't want to force you out," Dad adds with a chuckle. "I thought I was going to have to wait until you retired to be able to go to that beach in Florida for the summer."

"Are we both seriously talking about leaving Harvest Hollow?"

He frowns at me. "Of course not. I'll never actually leave here; this will always be home, at least for me. But I would like to vacation more." He winks at me. "Who knows, maybe I'll even have a daughter in Colorado that I can go visit. I know I'd like to go visit Kara in Vermont. And you can always come home and visit here."

"Wow. I feel like I sat down to tell you I'll eventually move out, but instead you're kicking me out. I see how it is," I say dryly. "You don't want me around here!"

"Not if you're all work and no play," Dad shoots back.

"Whose side are you on?" I fold my arms across my chest and try to glare at him. Hard to do while I'm lying on his leather couch.

"My own."

"I honestly can't imagine leaving Harvest Hollow forever. I really do love it here. I think that's why I haven't pursued something different yet. Because I'm genuinely happy here. But if I could go try something else for a few months? Just to get a taste of the outside world? That would make me really, really happy."

Dad chuckles. "You've been listening to Tripp talk about his travels, haven't you?"

I smile at him. "Yeah. And it reminded me that I used to dream about seeing different states as well. Never actually leaving here—but just experiencing more of the world, if you know what I mean."

"I think I do. Now why don't you relax and enjoy some time with Tripp while you plan this banquet?"

I slowly sit up and spin to face him. "That reminds me: what aren't you telling me? Because I know you and Tripp have something you're not saying," I accuse.

"You mean the part where I thought I was having a heart attack, but it turns out it was a panic attack?"

All teasing aside, I leap up and stare at him.

He holds up a hand. "It's fine. I went and visited the good doctor, and he helped me. It's why he volunteered both of you to help plan things."

"I didn't know I was pushing you so much!"

"You're not. Hazel. It's time for both of us to make some changes in our lives. I needed some stress off my shoulders. You need something. Maybe a change; it's up to you, but we're both getting pretty stagnant here, aren't we?"

I nod but don't say anything.

Dad continues, "It's time for us to find something that makes us happy—or at least at peace, don't you think?"

"Yeah, yeah, I do."

But finding that happiness and hanging on to it? That's a different ballpark altogether.

Chapter 28

Tripp

The parking lot is half-full—the benefit of coming on a school night. Most of the kids are at home and in bed. Now we won't have to pretend to have it all together in the haunted corn maze. We'll be free to scream at will.

"I'm so excited." Hazel looks at me with an evil glint in her eye. She was the one who texted me saying she was going to go to the haunted corn maze with or without me.

I pretend to check my texts, but really, I'm rereading hers.

Hazel: I'm going to the haunted corn maze tonight to celebrate surviving my first magazine shoot. If you're worried you'll pee your pants, please stay home. My friendship only goes so far.

Hazel: Daisy and Aria are busy and Mia refuses. I neeeeeeed you.

Hazel: Pls let me know ASAP. I might text the cute hockey player if you're not coming.

And so, even though I was exhausted after my shift, I pulled on a pair of jeans—they really aren't easy to button with one injured hand—and boots.

Now I'm standing in the Harvest Farms parking lot with Hazel again.

Hazel smiles brightly at me, the parking lot lights glowing in her eyes. "I promise to trip you and run if anything too scary shows up."

"Who says I'm not planning to do the same to you?"

Her jaw drops, and she clutches her hands to her chest. "And I let you be my number one best friend! Your privileges are being revoked. You're number two."

"I'll have to call Archie. Tell him we're in good company together." I bump her shoulder with mine as we walk toward the ticket booth. "Oh look? The demon goat!"

I point behind her, trying to distract her so I can hurry over and buy some tickets.

A hand latches on to the back of my jacket.

"Oops, did I already buy the tickets while I was waiting for you?"

I turn around to find her waving two tickets through the air like a fan. "Hazelnut."

We had decided to save time and meet each other here, so she must have beat me by a few minutes.

"Shall we?"

She seems happy—carefree. That must mean the World

Mechanic interview went well. She hasn't said anything about it yet, but I know she will when she's good and ready.

We pass our tickets to a teenager wearing a straw hat and a clown mask, then enter the haunted corn maze.

"I'll lead the way." Hazel practically cackles.

"Oh, sweet mustard, we'll have to live in this corn maze."

We walk forward to the first split in the path, and Hazel reaches back to pinch my arm.

I don't know if it's because I've recently realized I'm attracted to her, or if it's always been this way, but I'm now hyper-aware of every single time she touches me. Picking her up in the pumpkin patch had been a mistake. All that's been replaying in my mind is the feel of her warm body against mine, and that is not how a best friend is supposed to feel.

We've always been comfortable with each other. She probably hasn't changed a thing. It's just my perspective. Yup, that's exactly what it is. A new outlook on life.

But as we go through the maze and creepy clown after zombie jumps out, she moves toward me and latches on in some way. It's almost subconscious, but each time she does it, she hangs on a little longer. Pretty soon, I'm wrapping her up in my arms and holding her there longer.

She doesn't seem to mind, so I decide to test a theory. A theory in which I can let go of her easily, because I'm not *that* attracted to her.

I point behind her and scream.

Some men think it's not manly to scream. I don't know if it's right or not, but I've never had to pretend with Hazel and I'm not starting now.

She doesn't even look behind her; she jumps into my

arms, wrapping her legs around my waist and starts screaming with me. "Run!"

Turning left, I wrap my arms around her waist, letting my good hand do most of the lifting, and do my best to run with Hazel as an attachment. By the time we get to the dead end, we're both gasping with laughter.

Except it *is* difficult to let go of her. And it completely disproves my theory that it was a glitch in my system. *I want Hazel in my arms.*

"You faker!" she accuses. "I didn't see anyone." But then there's a clown face peering at us through the cornstalks. I spin around so she can see it, and this time, she's the one starting the screaming while the clown walks past us with a maniacal laugh.

Hazel leans back and smacks my shoulder but remains in my arms. New level unlocked. Maybe Hazel does like being held by me.

I'm forced back to the present by an angry blue gaze and a fireball in my arms. "You know I hate clowns jumping out of dark places!"

"We're in a haunted corn maze. There are going to be creepy clowns." I chuckle.

She unlocks her legs, and I lower her to where her feet are on the ground again. She grins up at me.

There's no doubt about it. I'm attracted to my best friend. But what am I going to do about it?

And an even more important question: does she feel the same?

Chapter 29

Tripp

Unfortunately, I haven't had the chance to answer either question because after the corn maze, I worked a twenty-four-hour shift, then crashed in bed and slept for eight hours straight, and now I'm meeting with Hazel to finalize the valet parking plan.

We're meeting at her usual spot—Cataloochee Coffee. But when I see her standing in front of the store in the cold fall air, I know something is wrong.

"You don't look so good, Hazel," I tell her. I really hope that she just brushes me off and tells me that she's fine. But the way she's standing there—looking at the front door of the coffee shop? Not moving? It's not a good sign.

She slowly turns to look up at me. "I'm just thinking."

I look at her skeptically. "Thinking?"

"I had an offer from *World Mechanic* to intern at a shop they own. I'm thinking about it. I'm fine." Her voice is hoarse. "Stop worrying."

She's shaking. She's obviously *not* fine. Her eyes are red.

Pretty sure she has *not* been contemplating her life choices right now.

I step forward and press a hand to her forehead.

"Oh, heck, Hazel. You're burning up."

She shakes her head once. "I'm fine. I need some caffeine."

"You do not need caffeine right now."

She tries to glare up at me, but it almost looks like it's too much energy to move her eyebrows. "Why are you standing out here on the sidewalk if you're fine?"

"I'm waiting for someone to open the door."

Glancing back and forth between her and the door, I ask, "You're waiting for someone to open the door?"

"Yes, because it kind of hurts to move right now. And I'm not sure why."

"I can tell you why. You're in denial. Just like you always are when you're sick. Hazel, you can get sick. You are not superhuman."

"I'm willing it away. Mind over matter. I don't have time to be sick."

I sigh. So like Hazel. She had influenza during her senior year volleyball state championship. She refused to quit because she was the best player on the team. They needed her. They won. And then she was sick in bed for a week afterward. She's the ultimate denier of sickness. But when she *does* get sick, she goes the distance and scares everyone close to her.

"You are going home and getting in bed."

"So, you're talking dirty now." But her teasing doesn't even come across that way because her words are whispered. She still hasn't moved besides the trembling.

There's a slight hunch to her shoulders. "Where did you park?"

"In the park."

"That's two blocks away." I glance down the block to see that most of the street parking is completely full.

"I know; I didn't want to pay for parking," she groans. "I'm trying to figure out how I'm going to get back there. After my coffee, of course."

She takes a slow step forward and hugs her arms around her chest. I shake my head and walk over to her.

I take off my jacket and wrap it around her. She closes her eyes as the extra layer of warmth envelops her.

"I'm taking you home, and I'm putting you in bed. And feeding you hot soup and Tylenol." She gives a barely perceptible nod.

"Okay." And that's all I need to know about how sick Hazel is. If she's willing to let someone take care of her, she's pretty sick. My car is parked at the end of the block, in the metered parking lot because I don't hold grudges like Hazel.

"We'll come back for your car," I assure her. "I know a guy who tows cars."

Then I scoop her up into my arms and start walking down the sidewalk toward my car.

Hazel doesn't even fight me on it, simply leans her head against my shoulder as we walk down the sidewalk. "Are you going to hurt your hand?"

"I'm keeping the injured side pointed away. Besides, it's healing quick," I reassure her, even though it's not healing as fast as I'd hoped.

"You're going to embarrass us. But it might be more embarrassing if I crawl down the sidewalk," she confesses.

"Don't worry, no one's getting embarrassed. You'll give me a great chance to show off my muscles," I tease.

She doesn't even laugh—simply snuggles closer. "You're probably going to get sick from me."

"Don't be such a pessimist. I work in an emergency room. I've already been exposed to this. I'm amazed you lasted this long with the flu going around town."

"My hectic social life keeps me from getting sick."

We make it to the car. I slide her into the passenger seat, then hurry to the driver's side.

Part of me wonders if I should take her to the hospital to get fluids, but I know that if she wakes up to me carrying her into the ER, she'll murder me. And refuse to be admitted. So, until I know that it's a dire situation, I'll take care of it myself. If I can keep fluids in her, she should be fine.

I can only hope. Because if she ends up getting dehydrated and needing to go the hospital for an IV? She'll be beyond angry.

After Hazel gets buckled in, she leans her seat back and tries to get comfortable.

It's not ideal, but I decide to stop at the market to get a bunch of electrolyte drinks and over-the-counter medicine before I take her home.

"What are we doing?" Hazel asks as she weakly lifts her head to look around the parking lot.

"Grabbing sick supplies."

"Should I come in with you?" she asks.

Before I have the chance to answer her, she looks at the Publix storefront, the same one I ran into her at a couple weeks ago. "Oh, never mind. I don't shop here anymore. Do you want to take my card?"

"You know, they won't even remember the tampon incident."

She flops her head onto its side. "I'm probably the brunt of every lunch break joke at the store."

I nod solemnly. "Most likely. And I'm not taking your card. I've got this one. Lock the doors after me."

I climb out and wait until I hear it lock.

I try to be as fast as I can. Whatever this is, I know she's not prepared for it. She thinks she's superhuman, so her medicine cabinet consists of Band-Aids. I grab some acetaminophen and ibuprofen, along with a thermometer. She felt hot when I was carrying her back to the car. I wouldn't be surprised if she already has a raging fever.

By the time I get back to the car, she's awake and looking at me like I'm a stranger. I knock on the window and point at the lock.

She slowly hits the unlock button.

I open the door and climb in.

"Are you kidnapping me?" she whispers in a shocked voice.

"Yes, and I'm taking you somewhere dangerous."

"Where are you taking me?"

"Bed."

She might have been feeling like an elephant was tap dancing on her head, but she still had enough energy to raise her eyebrows at my poor choice of a word.

I can't believe I might actually be blushing.

"That's not—it's not—I didn't mean—"

She tips her lips up in a sad imitation of a smile as she closes her eyes and presses the side of her face against the window. "That's okay. I've always wondered which side of the bed you prefer. Maybe I'll find out someday."

Now I'm *definitely* blushing because I know that she doesn't mean it the way it sounds. But now it's out in the open.

I can't unhear it. Hazel's thought about sleeping with me.

Chapter 30

Tripp

I manage to get her upstairs into her apartment without too many incidents. She's usually strong, which is why it's so concerning that she doesn't mind that I am carting her up a flight of stairs. Regular Hazel would be freaking out.

"I'm hot," she mumbles as she fumbles with her keys.

"Here, let me take those." I pull them from her hand and unlock the door.

It is not hot outside. Time to get her comfortable in bed with some medicine and liquids.

"I don't like being sick, Tripp," she cries, full-on wail of defeat as she slumps against the door.

"I know, baby." I don't know how or why that slipped out, but I'm going to ignore it, especially since she is. I pull her against my chest and open the door, helping her walk inside.

She stumbles toward the bedroom, not even bothering to kick her shoes off.

I follow after her and pull back the covers. She sits down

on the edge of the bed, and I pull her shoes off, then her coat and scarf. I grasp the back of her head and gently lay her down on her pillow.

"I'm cold."

I start pulling layers of blankets over her. Piling them high as she shivers uncontrollably.

This isn't uncommon, I tell myself over and over again. This is classic viral flu symptoms. I deal with this all the time. Yet seeing Hazel suffer? It hits a little differently.

It's personal.

"It's okay. I'll be right back."

I mad-dash out to the car and come back up the stairs with the bags of groceries.

By the time I get back in her room, she's hot again and on top of the covers, sweating.

"I can't decide. Hot. Cold. Everything hurts," she mutters.

"Here, take this." I pass her some pills and then a bottle of an electrolyte drink.

She slowly swallows them, and I make sure she takes a few extra sips of the drink.

Her hand is shaky as she passes the bottle back. "Thank you, Tripp. You're the best."

With that, she finally snuggles under the covers and drifts off into a fitful sleep.

Thirty minutes later, she's tossing and turning.

I move to sit on the bed next to her. She rolls toward me and reaches a hand toward me. I grasp it and hold it gently.

She turns her hand to weakly squeeze back.

"Hazel," I whisper. "Hazel, it's okay."

"I know. You're always there when I need you."

"I'll always be there for you, Hazel." I mean it from the bottom of my heart.

"You're hot." Her hand reaches shakily for my face and her thumb lands on my lips. "Do you want a secret?"

"I think you're getting delirious..." I mumble against her finger.

"I've wondered what it would be like to kiss you."

With that, her hand drops back down to the bed, and she closes her eyes.

The next hour is spent going back and forth from cooling rag to heavy blankets and trying to get her to drink cold liquid without choking.

She finally settles into deep sleep, and I'm left sitting in a chair watching her.

Seeing her like this makes my chest hurt, so I do my best to imagine the corn maze night. The way she seemed so carefree, happy and kept jumping into my arms. Rattling on and on about every detail of the *World Mechanic* interview.

I've got to stop staring at her. So, I do the only thing I can think of. I pick up the mystery book lying on the nightstand next to the lamp. Maybe if I make myself miserable reading, I'll stop imagining kissing my best friend.

I stay all day, and then the entire night.

Biff knocked on the door midafternoon, wondering where Hazel was, and then promptly abandoned us when he found out she had the flu and that I was willing to take care of her.

Her fitful sleep calmed by midnight, and she seemed to

be on the brink of cracking through the fever. Now, I spent part of the time is lying next to her, holding her when she's cold and the rest of the time I'm sitting in the chair reading.

When morning rolls around, I'm back in the chair.

Hazel groans and stretches and glances at the clock on the wall.

When Hazel turns to look at me, her eyes are clear. The fever is gone, and she looks actually cognizant.

"What happened?"

I toss the book onto her bed. "It was *not* the butler."

She stares at the book for a few seconds before she wiggles to sit upright. "You read my book." Her tone is incredulous.

"Yup."

She looks at me slowly. "Did you like it?"

I smirk at that. "As much as it pains me to admit it, you were right. It was actually really fun to read."

She smiles softly. "I knew eventually I'd get you to crack. I just didn't know it would take getting the flu from hell."

I stand up, pick up the thermometer, and walk over to sit on the bed. I brush her hair away from her face and scan her forehead.

"I didn't know I had that." She looks pointedly at the thermometer.

"You didn't. I grabbed it from the store when I picked up Tylenol. You are not prepared for any kind of sickness. All I found in your cabinet was cough drops and whiskey."

"See? A fully functioning medicine cabinet."

I scowl at her. "You worry me. Now sit up some more so I can get you to drink some fluids."

"I don't think I like bossy Tripp." The little minx actually sticks out her tongue at me.

"Well, you better get used to it because someone has to remind you to take care of yourself."

"And here I was thinking how nice you were for taking care of me while I was sick. I should have known the real you would show up. And here you are..." she complains.

"And here I'm going to stay." What Hazel doesn't know is that I mean it in more ways than one.

Chapter 31

Hazel

Three days after the flu, and I'm still staring at the Post-it notes Tripp left.

If you're feeling <u>hot</u>, make sure you drink lots of liquid.

You kissed that flu pretty good. Make sure you don't overdo it.

Another Post-it note I found on my front door.

I swear if you relapse because you're working too hard, you're going to be in big trouble with me.

. . .

It's not so much the notes that make me break out in hives... but the emphasis he put on certain words. Like underlining the word hot. Or spacing the word kissed a little oddly.

I try to remember everything I said when I was sick, and there's a sinking feeling in my stomach that all those fever dreams...might not have been a dream.

To make matters worse, I have a text from Eli today.

Eli: I picked out the perfect tie to match your eyes...but...

Hazel: but? That feels like a big but

Eli: Oh, I definitely have a big 'but'

Hazel: lol

Eli: Found out I've got an extra practice before the big game on Saturday. I wish I could be your date to the benefit dinner.

Hazel: It's all good! I completely understand.

And while I understand, that still means I will have zero buffer between Tripp and me and this attraction that's growing stronger by the second.

The man held my while I had the influenza. How could my attraction *not* grow?

Luckily, I have a morning coffee hangout session with Floyd, Henry, and Jean. They're all men. They can help me figure out where I went wrong and how to repair the damage, because they'll understand what Tripp is thinking.

I make record time getting to the coffee shop and charge inside, not bothering to order a coffee.

"We have an emergency," I say as I flop down in the empty chair next to Jean.

"What now?" Floyd leans forward and picks up his coffee cup as he waits for my answer.

"It's definitely an emergency," Henry says. He points at the empty table. "She didn't even get her coffee yet."

"I got the flu."

Everyone's chairs scrape as they scoot as far away from me as they can.

I wave a hand through the air. "I'm not contagious anymore. I wouldn't do that to you guys."

Floyd nods and scoots his chair forward again. "So, what's the problem?"

"Tripp took care of me while I was sick."

Jean lets out an evil chuckle while Henry waggles his eyebrows back and forth.

"And the problem is?" Floyd asks.

"I may or may not have said some incriminating things while I had a fever."

Floyd sighs. "How many times do I have to tell you never admit to anything."

"It's sound advice." I nod frantically. "I can pretend like it didn't happen."

Henry's shaking his head. "What did you say to him?"

I take a minute to look at all three faces. How did my girls' group turn into this? Doesn't even matter. They're wonderful, and I need them.

"I told him that I thought he was hot."

"Maybe he thought you meant temperature," Jean helpfully suggests.

"Yeah, and maybe he didn't hear me when I said I'd like to kiss his face."

Everyone grimaces at that.

"Yeah. It's bad. Irreparable bad."

Everyone sits in silence, and the new barista comes over

with a coffee for me. "Samantha told me this is your regular drink."

"Aww, thank you," I say and pull out my card to pass to her. She smiles and disappears behind the counter.

"Okay. All right. I have it figured out." Floyd nods sagely. "First, you tell him you once dated a man that looked like him. And you imagined that he was him while you had a fever."

I press my lips together as I warm my hands on the hot cup of coffee. "That's actually pretty good."

"Did you say his name?" Jean asks.

"Maybe? I don't think so, though. No. Definitely not."

Henry grins. "You probably said his name, and now he can't get you out of his head."

"Henry. Stop reading romance novels."

"You can't shame my reading choices," he admonishes.

I chuckle. "Touché. I love that you read romance. But real life is not a romance novel! Me telling my best friend that I'm attracted to him is going to end up with me being friendless."

Everyone at the table glares at me in unison. "What are we, chopped liver?" Henry pipes up.

"You're all above friend level. I'm trying to earn my way into your inner circle because you're way cooler than me."

Jean nods. "It's true. We are. We went to a Taylor Swift concert this year, and you didn't."

I lean forward and lay my head down in my arms as I shake with laughter. I can never keep up with these three, and I've never been so grateful for them.

Finally catching my breath, I sit up. "Okay. I like Floyd's

idea about mistaken identity. It's solid. Believable. It gives me some creative license."

They all look at me like it is absolutely not going to work. I'm going to have to make it work. Or else.

Or else I'll have to flee the country. Or at least the county.

I pick up my cup of coffee and take a long sip. The perfect temperature. Time to wash my worries away.

"Did you get that clutch replaced on the old Ford?" Jean asks.

And now our conversation is back into the nice happy territory again. Much safer. Clutch replacement and engine problems.

I can talk about that all morning if it will distract me from my boy problems.

Chapter 32

Tripp

Tripp: I need help.

It's a lifeline. I've been staring at the kitchen wall.

The green tile stares back at me as I recall the last seventy-two hours. I just got off a very busy work shift and I'm taking time to process.

But this time I'm not having to decompress from work. Instead, I'm thinking about something else: Hazel being sick. Hazel telling me she'd like to kiss me. Or at least, I think that's what she was implying. There was a lot of room for interpretation. Like maybe she wouldn't kiss me, even though she wanted to? I need a professional's opinion on how to handle this.

And who better than the man who got married twice to the same woman? He's had lots of practice deciphering what women mean when they say something.

Archie responds within five minutes.

Archie: Anything. What do you need?

Archie, while being best friend number 2, is a good friend. One I was happy to help get back together with his ex-wife. Although he'd been the one to come up with the original win-back-Meyer plan, his plan hit a little speed bump when he crashed his plane and got amnesia. Luckily, I was there to keep things on the right track.

My romantic roots run deep.

Tripp: What if I'm attracted to my best friend?

Archie:...

The dots disappear, then reappear just before his text comes through.

Archie: I appreciate the compliment, but I am happily married.

Of course, Archie would go there, which is why he isn't best friend number one. He doesn't know how to read my mind like Hazel does, which is scary to think about. What if she knows I find her attractive?

Tripp: I'm not talking about you.

Tripp: It's about Hazel

Archie: oooooooh, Your #1 best friend?

Tripp: Yeah, that's the one.

Archie: ?

Tripp: I can't stop thinking about her.

Archie: Is she single?

Tripp: Yes.

Archie: Well, that's good, I guess.

Tripp: You're not being very helpful.

Archie: Have you told her yet?

Tripp: NO. I don't want to ruin our friendship for the rest of our lives.

Archie: So, your friendship is still strong? I thought maybe I was cracking it the other day when I talked to her.

Tripp: It's on shakier ground right now, so I don't want to do anything to mess it up.

Archie: What if it's on shakier ground because she thinks you're hot, too? You're not kids anymore.

Tripp: Thank you, Captain Obvious. But we weren't kids when I left for college either.

Archie: You were eighteen. You were still a kid mainly being run by hormones.

Archie is officially unhelpful. But he did bring up a good point. Our friendship *has* been strained ever since I came back. What if it's because she's experiencing the same feelings as me?

Maybe her fever dream came from a very real place of being attracted to me?

Biff texted me right after I finished touring that old house for sale.

It's a sprawling four bedroom on an acre lot. The house is outdated and there hasn't been much landscaping done in a very long time...but the price is right.

I gave the real estate agent my offer, so now I'll wait to hear back if the owners will accept it or not.

I unlock my phone when I climb into the car.

Biff: Could you and Hazel go look at the venue today? Make sure everything is in order for the big day?

I text Hazel and ask when she wants to go.

Hazel: I'll come to you.

Thirty minutes later, we're going through a drive-through donut shop while she's talking on speakerphone with Milo explaining where she set the cheater bar.

She hangs up and picks up a giant donut. "Sounds like everything is set for the valet service. How's your donut?"

I look down at my regular-sized maple bar. "Less likely to send me into a diabetic coma."

"But you don't have diabetes."

"Yet. Type 2 can happen at any time in life."

"You and your doctor facts trying to ruin my donut. Something else will get me first." She steps on the gas and shoots through an intersection on a very yellow, slightly red light.

"Yeah, like that truck that almost hit you," I mutter.

"What was that?"

"Oh nothing, just wondering why I didn't fight you for the driver's seat."

"Because you'd lose?" she asks sweetly as she turns onto Maple Street.

I rest an arm across the back of her head rest and ask her in a low voice, "You sure about that?"

"Oh look, metered parking!" Hazel points out the passenger side window as she steps on the gas and speeds by. "Not today, Satan!"

"You realize we're going to have to walk..." I ask as she continues toward the city parking lot.

She dodges a squirrel—they are prolific and thriving downtown—and turns onto the side street that leads to the city park parking lot. She pulls in, parks the car, and jumps out. "Okay. Come on. We're going to time it to see how long it takes to walk."

"Are you going to do valet parking for everyone?"

"No, only for the people who aren't able to find a parking spot close. Let's hoof it, brother."

I groan inwardly, "Please don't ever say that again."

"What, 'hoof it?'" she asks as she locks the car and starts walking back in the direction we came.

"No. 'Brother.'"

"Too familial for you?" She gives me a long look and then asks, "Bestie?"

"Hmm. Or something."

Her laugh trickles back to me as she speedwalks forward.

"Are your valets going to be walking this fast?"

"Probably not," she admits as she slows down.

"That's better." I finally catch up to her. She might be short, but she's mighty, especially when determined.

I can't help but stare at her as we turn onto Maple. Her cheeks are flushed from the cold—not a fever, and her eyes are sparkling. Her big headband is holding back waves of blonde hair.

Her jacket is pulled close under her chin as though she doesn't dare allow any cold in.

She catches me staring at her and asks, "What are you looking at?"

"You."

She misses a step, and I shoot out a hand to steady her.

Her slender fingers wrap around mine, and she grasps my hand firmly.

"Um, er, a pothole."

"There wasn't a pothole."

I want her to turn and look at me. To tell me that she doesn't feel what I feel. But she continues forward toward the venue.

But she doesn't let go of my hand.

When we reach the entrance of the venue, she enters the number code on the hand-carved wood door, which is surrounded by a narrow section of white brick. We enter the foyer, where a wide wooden staircase leads upstairs to the ballroom. Just to the left of the staircase is an elevator.

"Is this wide enough for a valet system?" Hazel asks.

"You know, they never covered that in medical school."

Hazel jerks her hand out of mine and smacks my chest. "Don't be ornery."

"Yeah, I think this entryway is huge. My apartment could fit in a quarter of it."

"Ha, your apartment is probably the size of that elevator shaft."

"Now who's being ornery?"

The only time Hazel had been in my apartment was when she drove me home after I had my hand stitched up. She said she could understand why I was interested in buying a sprawling ranch style house.

"Okay, for the most important event of today," Hazel says slowly. "I'll race you to the top."

The little stinker runs for the elevator, and I'm left sprinting up the staircase.

Luckily, all that uphill hiking comes in handy, and I beat the elevator up by two seconds.

"What took you so long?" I ask as she steps off onto the hardwood floor. She ignores me because she's a poor loser.

"This obviously will work fine. We used this same space

last year, but I need to check on the staging areas. Like the kitchen and storerooms. Make sure they have everything they're supposed to."

The kitchen looks great. One of the storerooms is full of tables and chairs that come with the rental of this building, and then there's one more storeroom. Hazel snaps the light on and steps inside. "This must be the maintenance one, but I wonder if there's enough room in the back to store the door prizes."

I follow her inside as she moves past the shelves into the empty space.

Slam.

We both pivot to see that the storeroom door is closed.

"That scared me," Hazel exclaims.

"Hmm, must be a draft in this building." I take a step forward to open the door. I jiggle the handle. It doesn't budge.

I try lifting up while turning the handle, but that does nothing.

I lean my shoulder against the door and twist the nob furiously.

"Um, Tripp?"

"Yes, Hazel?" I mutter as I keep trying to open the door.

"Maybe that sign explains it."

Lifting my head, I follow her pointer finger to a paper sign taped to the wall next to the door.

Storage door locks automatically. DO NOT CLOSE IT.

That's when I'm forced to embrace the cold hard fact that Hazel and I are locked into a storeroom together.

The company couldn't be better.

"We're stuck," I inform her as I glance around taking in

our surroundings. Luckily, the light is still on, but there's only one way out of here.

She looks at me as though she's searching my face for signs of a joke.

Then she slams herself against the door. "I don't do small spaces! I'll perish in here."

I jump forward and pull her away from the door before she can hurt herself. I had never realized Hazel was claustrophobic. With her climbing under cars all the time, I figured she'd be fine, but she's shaking in my arms.

I turn her around so it will be easier to hold her...and realize that she's shaking with laughter.

"What the—"

She gasps as she tries to pull in a breath.

"Are you going hysterical?"

"No! Aria got me started watching Turkish Romcoms, and anytime the girl gets stuck somewhere she starts to panic, and of course, a gorgeous man is somehow trapped in there with her and helps her. I figured I'd give it a try for myself."

Her gasping laughter trickles off into an occasional giggle, and I smile down at her. "And how did that work out for you?"

"Well, here you are. You tell me?" she teases.

I freeze, swallowing the lump in my throat before I say, "Okay. Let me try."

"Seeing if a gorgeous man will come to save you?"

I look at her flatly. "No. Try seeing if I can open the door."

Five minutes later and the door has not budged. I tried the hinges. And every combination of jiggling and lifting the knob. Nothing works.

"Oh no. This is going to be mortifying to have to call for help."

"How so?"

"It makes the most sense to call the owners of this building, which are Don and Janet Douglas…"

I groan. Don Douglas is one of those self-important businessmen who thinks the entire world should know who he is.

"Yup. Harvest Hollow Happenings could strike at any moment."

"Hey, no hate on the Harvest Hollow Happenings Instagram page. It's how I've kept up with news the last few years."

Hazel looks at me flatly. "It's wildly inaccurate. I'd find a better news source."

"Okay then. We can't call the Douglases. Who would we call?" I ask. Everyone I know is at work right now. The downside of having irregular work hours.

"Dad," Hazel says. "It might take him a while, but at least we know he's home."

"Make the call."

A short phone call later, Biff says he's out on a tow call but that he will send some help our way. Hazel and I look at each other and groan, knowing that this can't end well for us.

"Maybe I should call Jean," she suggests.

"That's probably who your dad is calling."

"Good point." She spins around to take in the details of the storeroom while I sink down to the floor. Might as well get comfortable.

I watch in fascination as Hazel finds a screwdriver and begins trying to crack her way out of here.

That's when I remember that she referred to me as a gorgeous man.

I am the man from the Turkish show. That's essentially what she said. And she held my hand. And she's been blushing when I look at her.

Hello, missing puzzle pieces; thank you for finally lining up in Tripp's brain.

I'm not the only one in this room who's attracted to their best friend.

Chapter 33

Hazel

After a few fruitless minutes of trying to open the door, Tripp decides not to waste his time any longer. He sits down on the ground and leans against a locked cupboard.

I find a screwdriver on an open shelf and decide to try my hand at unlocking the door. Maybe I can unhook the knob from this side...

That doesn't work either. So, I slump back to the ground and spin the screwdriver over and over again in my hands, trying to figure out how to get out of here before some town busybody finds out about this.

But when Tripp asks me a question, I forget everything problem I'm trying to solve.

"Soooo...what's your favorite way to kiss?"

I drop the screwdriver. It clatters against the hardwood floor. The closet floor has lots of dents and scrapes already. One more dent won't make a difference.

"What did you say?" I ask as I sink to the floor and lean back against a stack of boxes.

Tripp unwraps a piece of gum from his pocket and pops it into his mouth. "Oh, you know. I was just curious how you liked to kiss."

Tripp has been my best friend for over fifteen years. In that time, we've never talked about physical things. Heck, we haven't talked about the details of any of our relationships unless it's to ask each other if we should break up. (The answer is always yes.)

Him asking how I like to kiss? This is new territory. And I don't know where he's going with this. Is he just being the Tripp I've always known? Or is this the new Tripp who recognizes the zap of electricity every time we touch?

"Uhn." My articulated reply makes Tripp smile.

"What are you talking about?" I shift uncomfortably against the boxes. Tripp pulls his knee up to his chest and rests his arm on it. He looks so calm. Asking a question like that? He must be joking if he's looking this calm. Or maybe I'm mishearing what he's really asking. Maybe this *is* typical best friend territory.

Maybe I'm supposed to ask him how he likes to kiss.

"You mean, how do I like to kiss my boyfriends?"

Tripp shakes his head. "I just figured we had all the time in the world. I'm here. You're here. We're stuck in this room together...maybe you'd like to tell me how you like to kiss."

I watch in fascination as his eyes travel down to my toes, then all the way back up to my face as he adds, "Or maybe show me."

And there it is.

There is no misunderstanding now. No guessing what his gaze means—especially that little smirk.

"Oh." I'm full of impressive words right now.

I'm so charming.

So self-possessed. Nearly drooling at the thought of kissing Tripp Sharpe. Something I've thought about for a lot of years. Something I never thought would ever come to fruition.

"I guess it depends on who's starting the kiss." Okay that's better. At least I don't sound too brassy.

"If you're starting the kiss?" He leans forward, and the storage room feels much smaller. He rests both arms over his knees, completely relaxed, as though this is a normal conversation for him. Who knows, maybe it is.

So, I mirror his stance and lift my eyebrows as I answer him, "It depends on who I'm kissing."

"Oh really?" Tripp scoots forward until his shoes bump against mine. "And what if you're kissing me?"

Good gravy and biscuits, he *went* there. "I don't know, I've never kissed you before. Are you a sloppy kisser?"

"Of course I'm not a sloppy kisser." He looks perturbed at the thought.

"I wasn't sure; you seem like a nice guy."

He narrows his eyes at me. "Nice guys are the best kissers."

"Have you kissed a lot of nice guys?" I ask. My voice is husky, like I've recently taken up smoking. Like I've smoked twelve packs today.

I might actually have to consider smoking in case Tripp's kisses are addictive. I'll need something to replace them.

He scoots forward. "Have you?"

ARStrokekESE

"One. He was a sloppy kisser and I'd prefer to not repeat the experience."

"You always say I'm a nice guy..."

"I think you're many other things as well." I fight a smile as I watch the emotions flash across his face.

"And what do *you* think I am, Hazel?"

I bite my top lip, debating how to answer him. As I search his face, waiting for him to save me from having to speak, I realize he's waiting me out.

"I guess I'm wondering if you're a good kisser."

"Why don't you find out?"

I scoot forward until our elbows are bumping each other. My legs are on the inside of his.

I lean forward and wait.

He doesn't move.

"What's this?" I ask.

He shakes his head once. "I'm waiting for you to show me how you like to kiss. Then I'll show *you* how I like to kiss."

"For a nice guy, you don't fight fair."

There's that low chuckle I'm starting to love. "I've never claimed to be the nice guy. That's the label you've given me."

And suddenly, I would like to find out exactly how much of a nice guy he is. How he kisses. If he'd be different with me than he is with everyone else—even in the way he kisses. Because I get to see the Tripp version that's sarcastic and funny and a lot of times, irreverent. I get the version that isn't the nice guy the rest of the world sees. I get the one who wants to figure out how to enjoy life.

I tuck my knees under me and lean forward, resting my hands on his arms. He doesn't move.

I move forward until I'm only a breath away from his lips.

No one's smiling now. This is serious business. This is the line in the sand that once we cross it, there's no going back.

There's no coming back from kissing your best friend. I feel the hitch of breath more than I hear it. His arms tense beneath my hands.

Leaning forward, I press my lips against his.

Our eyes are wide open. There's a slight scruff on his face that pokes my cheeks. He doesn't move. I stay frozen there. Feeling the fullness of his lips against mine. His breath matching mine. Afraid to move. Afraid this moment will end. So, I leave my lips matching his until I feel his bottom lip quiver and those arms shift.

"Is it my turn?" he murmurs against my lips.

"Just a minute," I mumble back.

Our lips bump against each other with each word we form. His lips are thinner than mine. But nice. He smells amazing. And I am now realizing exactly how long his eyelashes are. They put eyelash extensions to shame. He's staring at me as I keep my lips matched with his.

After a moment, I move my top lip to the side. And press a little kiss to the corner of his mouth.

"I'm not sure how much more of this I can take, Hazel." His voice is husky.

"One more minute." I lift one hand from his arm and move it to the back of his neck. I've wondered what it would feel like to run my hands through his hair back there. It's soft with a light curl. The back of his neck feels hard, strong. Tense. I feel his arms move to my back. Hard bands encircle my waist. I press a more intentional kiss against his lips.

"My turn," he says, as his arms tighten around me,

pulling me flat against his chest, my legs press out behind me. And the full weight of my body rests against Tripp.

"I knew you'd drive me crazy." And then his hand is at the back of my head, lacing through my hair.

Tripp's hand is in my hair.

Tripp's mouth is on mine.

And he tilts my head so that he can kiss me fully. He deepens the kiss, showing me just how Tripp Sharpe can kiss. He's very thorough. Leaving nothing unturned. Exploring every area of a kiss.

Well, if this is what kissing a nice guy is like, there's no going back. I'm going to need that pack of cigarettes.

Because one thing's for sure—I'll never be able to look at my best friend the same again.

Chapter 34

Hazel

A thump breaks through our haze, and we both pull back at the same time, our lips reluctant to part.

"What was that?" I whisper.

We wait a minute but don't hear anything else.

Tripp looks at me with a lazy smile on his face. "Probably my heart."

Oh gosh. He did not dive that deep that fast...

I leap to my feet.

"Tripp. Tripp, we can't. I can't lose you."

"You're not going to lose me," he says placatingly as he slowly stands up. His eyes have a haze over them and he's looking at me like he wants more.

"No. What we just did—" I point at the floor. "We can't do that again."

"Why not? I thought it wasn't that sloppy."

"Tripp! It will ruin our friendship, and I will not survive." I hiccup. "I will not survive losing you."

My words are finally getting through to Tripp. He looks

—hurt. Deflated. Confused even. I feel the same way, but one of us has to make the responsible choice.

"Why can't we play it out and see where it goes?"

"Because it would end with a fractured friendship," I try to explain desperately.

"And you think this won't change things?" he asks as he points at the same spot on the floor that I am.

"It's a blip. It was curiosity, nothing more. It's only natural that we would wonder. And now we know, and it's time to go back to normal."

"I can't—"

Tripp cuts himself off as we hear footsteps and a loud voice calling, "Which closet are you stuck in?"

After some clinking that must be a key in the lock, the door opens, and we look at the entrance, only innocence in my eyes. At least, as much as I can summon.

It's Annie Perkins standing there. Of course, she would be the one to find us in the closet. "Oh hello, I just came up because Biff said that you were up here," she says with a smile.

I slip my hands into my jacket pockets. "Thanks for opening the door. For some reason, it locked behind us."

We hurry and walk out of the closet—storeroom, whatever the space is.

They really should have a lock on the inside of the door so that people can get out. I'll have to have the owners look into it before the benefit dinner.

Seems like some sort of a safety hazard for a staging room. Against fire code, that's for sure. When we walked into the main room, I see Daisy standing there.

"Hey, Daisy," I greet her.

She grins at me, then looks to Tripp.

Annie stops in between us. "I'm so glad you're here. I've been meaning to introduce Daisy to Tripp. I think they would make a lovely couple."

My eyes widen at that, and I glance at the man I made out in a storeroom with. I want to scream at him that he's mine. I have a sudden urge to end my friendship with Daisy.

But none of that happens.

"Now Hazel, I'd like to show you where the tablecloths are stored. I helped at a wedding here last month and it took us forever to locate them," Annie says as she drags me away. I hardly get a chance to look at Tripp.

Chapter 35

Tripp

Hazel's look is comical. Her wide blue eyes might be shooting daggers if she were capable.

But she's the one who decided we needed to keep it casual. She's the one who said that we couldn't let it go beyond that kiss.

Which is a joke.

Because I will never ever be able to look at her the same. I knew I was running that risk when I kissed her. When I even brought up the topic.

We could've gone on pretending for the rest of our lives, but now we know exactly what it's like to kiss each other.

We know exactly what the other one feels like.

There is definitely no going back.

And Annie Perkins's attempt to set me up with her niece right now, because that's exactly what she's doing, is a wasted effort. I will never get Hazel out of my mind.

Because what I've just realized? She's a once-in-a-lifetime.

That soulmate I've been looking for? I couldn't find her because I already had her.

And I don't want to let this chance pass me up. I'm going to do everything I can to convince her that we stand a chance.

Daisy smiles up at me with a twinkle in her eye.

Annie pulls Hazel to the side and is explaining something about tablecloths. Hazel glances at me over her shoulder, but her eyes land on Daisy. The hurt in her eyes makes me want to reach out to her, but Annie pulls her farther away.

"So, you're Annie Perkins's niece?" My attempt at conversation is completely lacking.

"More importantly, I'm Hazel's friend." She smiles blandly at me. "And as Hazel's friend, I hope you don't misunderstand me when I say, I'll wreck you if you hurt her."

I jerk my head in surprise. "If I, what? I thought—" I point at her and then me.

Daisy practically rolls her eyes. She *must* spend a lot of time with Hazel if she's picked up that habit.

"You've had Hazel so confused ever since you moved back to town. And you also have her lipstick on the corner of your mouth." Daisy keeps smiling but folds her arms across her chest. "I'm saying I would hate for you to do something to hurt her."

"She doesn't want anything with me," I admit.

"Maybe she doesn't know she *can* want something with you."

Chapter 36

Hazel

I thought that planning the benefit dinner wouldn't be that hard. My sister Kara did it for years. Dad did it last year. And now that it's my turn? I'm wondering if I could jump on a boat and sail for the Caribbean.

How dare Tripp tell me that he wants us to be something? I'm still mad at him for crossing that line.

Who am I kidding? I took a running leap over that line. But now I have to figure out how to tuck all those uncomfortable emotions back into a box. Because I have too much to do.

I have two job offers I'm seriously contemplating, along with an internship with a World Mechanic shop to get my L3 certification. Not to mention I have a banquet dinner to pull off.

Given the number of inane questions I've been asked...I can assume I'm a terrible communicator.

My only hope is that tonight—the much-awaited

banquet night—will be so busy that I don't have to deal with Tripp. I can't handle any more right now.

"Am I early?"

I spin around from where I'm laying out the final seating arrangements. Everything is mapped out carefully.

Aria is standing right behind me wearing a one-shoulder navy-blue dress that hits the floor.

Her long hair reaches nearly to her waist in braids.

I didn't ask her to help set up early, but she acts like she's supposed to be here. The banquet doesn't start for an hour.

"I'm so sorry. Did I text you the wrong time?" I say by way of greeting as I set down the cards and reach out to hug her, careful to not touch her hair.

"Were you tricking me into being here early to help? Because you know you could have just asked." Now she looks skeptical. Smart girl.

I grin. "That was purely a happy accident. But the banquet doesn't start until seven. Did I tell you it was six? How like me. Hopefully I didn't tell everyone that." I glance around in a panic.

"I don't mind. I'm just glad I'm on time. I was worried I wouldn't make it back from my hairdressers in time."

"Well, it looks gorgeous."

She runs a hand over the airspace of the beautiful braids. "Eight hours in the chair."

"Holy... Do you need a bag of ice to sit on?"

She laughs. "No, but standing sounds great. I'll help you with whatever you need."

We get to work laying out numbered cards next to each plate.

"So, you're sure this date auction is going to be fun?" Aria asks.

"I promise it is. And I'm sorry I was not very organized at getting information out there. The date auction was a fun last-minute addition, and I really am hoping it will be low-stress for everyone."

"Because that's what dating is for most people," she says with a raised eyebrow.

I glance at the DJ who's setting up the speakers and testing the feedback. The wait staff has arrived and they're looking around like they don't know the difference between a dining hall and a kitchen. The valets are here as well.

"Hazel!" And that would be the chef poking his head out. And the lighting man has arrived with a large cart on wheels.

I glance back at Aria, who I realize is watching my quiet internal breakdown. "Are you okay?"

I shake my head once. "So. Much. To. Do."

We're quiet as we watch the bustle of bodies bobbing around the room, not really accomplishing much. No one knows where they need to be. Because I haven't told them.

Because I hate organizing events.

But it's for a good cause, I whisper to myself.

Aria's quiet voice reaches me. "I would be happy to help with whatever you've got going on."

I don't even hesitate to grab at the lifeline offered to me.

"That would be wonderful. Would you mind laying out the rest of the cards and giving each valet one of these folders to read and sign?" I frown. "I'm sorry, I'm throwing all this at you, and you didn't ask for any of it."

She nods. "What are friends for? I can manage a few

valets after this school week. The kids are losing it thinking about all the Halloween candy coming up."

The knot in my chest eases. I didn't know how stressed I was going to be at this event.

I usually am. But this year has the added element of me being the one coordinating it.

How did Dad do this for years? No wonder he ended up in Tripp's ER. I wonder if I'll get there at some point too.

How am I going to face Tripp tonight? I'm the one who won't risk it...and I promised him everything would be the same, but I'm a big fat liar. I loved kissing Tripp. It was a moment when everything felt right in the world. But that's what it was: just a moment. I know I can't have that forever.

The only thing I can do is pretend. Like I have been ever since I saw him in that Publix with a tampon stuck in my hair.

Chapter 37

Tripp

Because Hazel was adamant about not needing my help early on the banquet night, I stayed away. But now as I reach the top of the stairs at the venue, I'm regretting that choice.

I missed out on a chance to talk with her before the guests started arriving. The room isn't full, but there are too many people around to have the conversation with Hazel that I wanted to.

"Hello, Miss Preston, you're looking lovely this evening," I say to Hazel. Because it takes everything in me not to say what I'm really thinking. *You look ravishing.* Delectable? Lots of words could replace lovely.

A scoop neck, lacy, blue dress that I know even without looking complements her eyes.

"You're not too bad yourself, Sharpe." She grins at me in such a casual way I would think our kiss didn't affect her. But when she taps a finger against the stem of my corsage, it's trembling. "What a big boy you are."

Teasing words that have a completely different meaning to me now.

I clear my throat and bite the comeback I have. "Are we the welcoming committee then?" I ask. "Do we have to go full regal and be bowing to everyone?"

She grabs the hem of the dress and curtsies deeply.

I latch on to her arm and pull her back up, but the movement brings her close to me, bumping her against my chest.

She looks up at me, startled. "How about you only curtsy to me?" I try to lighten my tone, but for some reason, it comes out grinding. I must be getting sick. That darn flu is circling back to get me out of spite.

"What's wrong with my curtsy?"

"Listen, you're not meeting the Queen of England, so there's no need to curtsy."

"I wouldn't curtsy for the current queen anyway."

I laugh. Of course she wouldn't. Hazel would probably pivot and curtsy to Kate out of spite if she ever ended up in that situation.

Hazel is just as at home in formal evening wear as she is in coveralls. Or at least that's how she looks.

But she acts as though she wears a form fitting dress every evening. Meanwhile, I can't tear my eyes off of her. So, we're going back to being friends. I don't know that I can actually do that.

"Now I have to go make sure the caterer has enough waitstaff." She turns around and sashays toward the kitchen, marching past the door that I know leads to a supply closet where I had an earth-shattering kiss.

Friends? With her? When I know how she kisses? Friends will never be enough. I want more.

"Dr. Sharpe, good to see you!" I spin around to greet Veda Banik, the new ER doctor who stitched me up.

"Dr. Banik. Good to see you too." I smile at her, then glance at the man beside her. "You must be Mr. Banik."

He smiles and extends a hand. "Yes, I am. Just got to town this weekend."

"Welcome to Harvest Hollow. I hope you can settle in soon."

"I'm actually a middle school teacher and I've been in contact with Annie Perkins. She's been great about helping us find housing. In fact, she offered to babysit the kids so that we could attend tonight." He looks slightly concerned at that last little bit, and Veda rests a reassuring hand on her husband's arm.

"Oh, you left the kids with the best person in town, don't worry. They'll have a great time. Sure, she might have them learning how to diagram sentences, but she'll make them like it at least."

They both laugh at that. "That puts Rohan at ease," Veda says with a smile. "Thank you for inviting us tonight. It feels like we're getting our first taste of the actual community here."

"I hope you enjoy yourself," I say as they try to find their seat.

Hazel is standing by the auction table. Picture displays of the item that's being sold and papers for people to write their bids on.

And then, the culmination of the evening: the part of the auction that has been buzzing around town ever since Hazel announced it on the social media pages. The Harvest Hollow Happenings has been buzzing with speculation about it.

The bachelor and bachelorette table.

A long table lined with men and women looking elegant in suits and formal dresses. Directly in front of each of them is a paper, and lots of chuckles and laughter fill the air as guests mill around bidding on a date.

Leave it to Hazel to come up with a way to add some fun to the event while still keeping it classy. Not parading the contestants in front of the entire banquet, but keeping it as a good-time kind of thing. I'm pretty sure she was able to get more help that way.

One chair at the end of the table is empty, but there's a piece of paper in front of it. I slide over there to look at the name on the paper.

It says Daisy.

Hazel's friend that I met after *the kiss.*

"Hazel told me that Daisy came down with the flu." I glance up to see that Adam is sitting in the seat next to the empty chair.

He's one of the bachelors for the night.

"So, she convinced you," I say, recalling the way I'd treated him the first time we'd met. Not one of my finer moments.

"She promised me it would make me feel like one of the locals." He raises both brows. "I'm not sure she was telling the truth, but it was very convincing."

I smirk at that. "She's good at that, for sure."

"Maybe we can convince her to be the missing date tonight," he suggests.

I throw back my head and laugh. "Good luck. If you can convince her, I'll be shocked."

Well, call me shocked because ten minutes later, Hazel's sitting at the table, smiling brightly as people start lining up to bid on a date with her.

Chapter 38

Hazel

I watch as Tripp greets a woman wearing a stunning golf dress. I wonder why she looks so familiar until I realize she's the new ER doctor. My stomach drops. Then I remember that she said something about having a husband. And now I'm mad at myself for the instant jealousy. I need a continual broadcast in my mind reminding me that Tripp and I can only be friends. I can't afford to mess things up with him. I need him.

I plant a smile on my face. Because I have to. I can't keep this facade up much longer. Hopefully I can fake it 'til I make it. Or break it.

Either way is fine as long as this torture ends. I'd like to scream out to the room that I kissed Tripp Sharpe. But they probably wouldn't believe me.

I cannot be around him alone again. I'll most likely jump all over him. Greeting him tonight took every ounce of self-control I possess.

"Hey, did you find a replacement for Daisy?" Dad asks as he stops beside me.

"No, I didn't."

"That's okay, sweetie. I saw that empty chair and was curious if someone else had filled it. I thought maybe you had," he says as he nudges my shoulder.

"Wait, me, fill it?"

He glances around to make sure no one is actually over-hearing us, and says, "Hey, listen squirt. I know you were hoping to have a date tonight. So why don't you go sit down over there and join in the fun? You could definitely use it after the year we've had. And with Tripp coming back."

"What about Tripp coming back?"

Dad shrugs. "I don't know. I guess I just always figured something would happen between the two of you. But I guess I was wrong."

I don't know if I should feel loved by my dad, or indulge in the ultimate pity party. Maybe both.

First the coffee crew, assuming marriage between Tripp and me. Then Aria and Daisy joking about his protective-ness. And now my dad saying something along those same lines.

Has everyone else but us been aware of what would happen?

And even though Dad's supportive of me spreading my wings, it's still going to just about rip my heart out to leave him. But giving my heart to Tripp and it not being enough for him? That would shatter me.

"How do you know these things?"

"Tripp called me yesterday and told me he'd like to date

my daughter. But if you don't feel the same way toward him..."

I slowly turn to stare at Dad with bulging eyes. "He what? He said that? Like he's asking permission?"

It takes everything to keep from shrieking.

"I'm not asking any questions," my dad says with a chuckle. "I don't want to know anything. But he was, in his words, 'clearing the air so I didn't have any surprises.'"

I take a deep breath. Given Dad's heart and stress levels, Tripp was being considerate by doing that.

"So why aren't you two thick as thieves tonight?" Dad continues to pry, even though he claimed he wasn't that interested.

"I was the one who ended it," I explain. Or didn't start it. Whatever.

"You were?" He sounded surprised. "You're way too much like your father, you know."

"Thank you."

"Not a compliment, kid." He scowls at me.

I scowl back at him. "What's wrong with being like you?"

"We're emotionally stunted. Risk averse in matters of the heart."

"Oh please, you know I'm not risk averse. Think of all the dumb stuff I've done in high school and college."

"I mean risk-averse in the big things. We don't like to risk our hearts. Did you know it was your mom who convinced me to take the risk? I didn't think we stood a chance, so I decided not to even risk asking her to marry me. I planned on keeping my love a secret and going our separate ways. She had different plans. The kind that involved latching on and having the love of a lifetime. And I see that with you and

Tripp. He's begging you to take that chance, and giving you every reason to be with him, and you're coming up with cowardly excuses."

With that, he turns and walks away into the crowd, looking annoyingly debonair in his black suit.

What a low blow to his own daughter. I'm *not* risk averse. This is for Tripp's own good. I don't want him getting hurt. I don't want to have to pick up my own shattered heart—

Fine. Maybe I *am* a little risk-averse on the emotional front.

But our situation is completely different than my parents'.

We have waaay more reasons why it couldn't work:

My parents: They came from opposite sides of the track.

Tripp and I grew up in the same small town.

My parents: They had a summer fling.

We've been best friends since childhood.

My parents: Mom was a debutante.

I'm a mechanic.

My parents: Mom moved states away,

And I want to do the same—but not for love.

Crap.

My parents really did beat the odds and I'm coming up with silly—but incredibly valid and logical— but still silly excuses on why I don't want to risk it with Tripp.

With an annoyed grunt that would not be considered ladylike, I walk over to the table where Adam sits next to the empty chair.

Daisy is gone with the flu, and I'd promised Adam he'd be sitting by someone fun. Unless he has an imaginary friend I don't know about, I haven't delivered on that promise.

Stopping along the banquet table, I greet everyone, hoping and praying I don't call them by the wrong names.

"Are you all doing okay?"

"It's going great!" Aria pops up and grins at me. "We're all competing to see who gets the highest bid."

Adam leans forward to look at her. "So did we all decide we're not allowed to bid on each other?"

He's staring at Aria in a warm, fuzzy way. Pretending like the two people sitting in between them don't even exist. Aha. Love is in the air.

"No, you have to play fair. We'd all be able to cheat and raise the bids just enough to beat people out. Besides, I'm on a teacher's salary. Unless these dates cost five dollars, then I'm out," she snorts, and I can't help but agree with her disgust.

"Oh, I'm not asking you to bid on mine," Adam says.

"I thought maybe you were embarrassed that no one was bidding on you," Aria teased.

This is entertaining. I'd like to sit down here all night and eat popcorn and watch these two go at it. I'm predicting wedding bells in eight months.

I look at the other four volunteers, and they all offer me game smiles, so I take it as a good thing and start to walk away.

"Hey wait!" Adam calls after me.

I spin around.

"Aren't you going to take Daisy's spot?"

"Um, no?"

He raises his eyebrows and stares at me. "Really? Are you scared?"

Too soon. Two people in one night accusing me of being a coward? That is not who I am. But that's who they see... "Of course not, I'm busy making sure everything is happening the way it should tonight."

He looks at the empty chair next to him. "It looks lonely."

"You look lonely," I shoot back.

Aria snickers.

"Aw well, Tripp said you wouldn't. I guess he was right."

I stiffen at that. Not because I'm one of those people who wants to be contradictory at every turn, but because I can't help but wonder why Tripp would say that.

I wonder if I wasn't clear enough. I do have to make it more obvious.

I need to show him that we'll be okay not dating.

And what better way than to do that by starting off at a date auction?

I walk around the table and flop into the chair.

I spin the paper around, cross out the name Daisy and write Hazel there.

"All better. Now, who wants to have a thrilling dinner conversation with me about the newest way I discovered to replace a catalytic converter?"

To my surprise, two gentlemen step forward from the line and write their bids down, one immediately after the other.

I grin at them both. "Thanks for saving my pride."

Somehow the faithful crowd that's been coming to this banquet all ten years has gotten wind that I'm here as part of the date lineup.

What fool thought up the idea to sell dates? The same one that's sitting in my chair. Me.

Dad walks by and laughs his head off as I glare at him. He's zero help.

A couple of men sign their names on the paper, and all I can think is that I'm about to bid on a date myself. I'll have to sell that old Ford GT, but I'll happily do it.

"Enjoying yourself?" Adam asks.

"I regret suggesting this. I'd like to personally apologize to each and every one of you on behalf of my ideas."

"I think it's pretty great." He glances over his shoulder toward Aria and then looks at me. "Besides. Aria said yes to going on a date with me, so I'm considering this evening a win."

Aria must be able to hear him because she leans forward and winks at me.

"Well good. Because I like both of you, and I always self-ishly want people I like to go on dates together so that I know they'll enjoy themselves."

Aria leans forward. "Do we get to read the bids?"

"Sure! Why not?"

We all flip our pages, and I stare at mine in shock. There are ten names on it. I hadn't realized there had been that many bidders, but I guess there was a crowd around the table.

"Wow! I didn't know it would go this well."

"Hey, you promised this would be amazing," Aria teases.

"I was hoping it would. Let's just say that," I tease back.

I glance up and spot Eli in the crowd. He has an easy-going smile on his face, and he's focused on me. Maybe this is exactly what I need to show Tripp that I'm over him. Even if I'm a hundred percent not.

I give him a little wave and he makes his way over hesitantly. He's probably worried I'll be upset about him not being my date tonight.

"You're here!" I exclaim.

"But late," he replies with chagrin. "How's my tie?"

I look at the dark blue tie he's wearing and press my lips together in a pout. "You know, I think that might match your eyes even better than mine."

He grins guiltily. "Pretty easy to match your eyes when I already have a tie matching mine..."

I laugh. "Well, I'm glad you made it anyway."

"Practice ended a little early and I couldn't resist coming to see you...but I see that you're auctioning off a date? So now I'm going to have to pay for the privilege?"

"Pretty much! It's along the lines of pay up or shut up, to get a date tonight," I say as I rest my chin on my hands and smile at him.

Eli grins down at me. "Pass me that pen."

Chapter 39

Tripp

After talking with Biff, I found a seat with Veda and her husband. I'm grateful I'll be working with her off and on from here on out. Usually, it's a struggle for me to make small talk, but with Veda, we have common ground: hospital gossip.

But I keep getting distracted watching Hazel sitting at the table talking to her endless line of admirers.

A blond man who looks familiar moves over to stand in front of her. He's grinning and chatting with her as he writes something on the paper.

I can't take it anymore. I stand up, the chair moving back with a loud scrape.

Dr. Banik looks at me with an amused smile.

"Not a word," I say.

She mimes, zipping her lips.

I move across the room, and as I get close, I hear the man say, "See? I wore a tie to match your eyes."

"I'm sorry tonight ended up looking different than we planned," Hazel replies.

"Well, hopefully, since they say bidding is about to close, it looks like we'll have another chance at a date."

I stop right next to him, glance down, and see a bid for $1500 for a date with her.

"I don't think so. She's mine."

I pick up the pen he just laid down and slide the clipboard in front of me.

Hazel's jaw drops open as I write my name in the empty slot slowly, that way, I can read the rest of the names on the roster.

Floyd. *Of course he would bless his heart.*

Wayne Oakley. *Pretty sure that guy is married.*

Hanson. *The guy just doesn't understand the word no.*

A couple of names I don't recognize.

And then the last bid.

Eli Hopkins. That's when I put two and two together. He's a hockey player for the minor league in town. I saw him play when I watched a game at the Summit Center.

I finish scrawling my name, then pause as I shift over to the amount I should bid. $1500? I double it.

Hazel gasps, and Eli chuckles. "I guess we won't be having that date after all." He gives Hazel a little wave. "I'll see you around, Hazel."

Hazel's eyes are still locked on me as she answers him slowly, "I'll, uh, yeah. See you around."

Eli leaves, and I'm left to face Hazel's shock all by myself.

"What'd he bid?" Her friend Aria leans forward to ask.

The man from the coffee shop leans forward to grab the clipboard and see. He lets out a low whistle as he says to

Aria, "We might only be able to afford one date together if this is the going price."

Aria gasps as he flips it around to show her.

Hazel stands up and plants her hands on the table as she tries to stare me down. She still has to look up at me. "This changes nothing, Tripp. We can't."

I lean forward and plant my hands on either side of hers and look down at her. "This changes everything, Hazelnut. This is a no-surrender situation."

She lifts her hand and points her finger in my face. "I won't let this ruin our friendship."

"Then don't. But if you think that one kiss satisfied me, you're dead wrong. And I think you're having the same problem."

A couple of gasps go up and down the table, and the man from the coffee shop chuckles. "See? Told you he was boyfriend material."

I glance at him briefly, and he smirks at me. "I was never your competition. I could see the way things were going."

"Well, thanks."

Hazel grabs my tie and tugs me back to look at her. "Tripp. Tripp, we can't."

"Hazelnut, are you scared?"

Her eyes widen. "I am absolutely not scared. That is not why I'm—" She's practically sputtering.

"So, you do like kissing me?"

"Of course I like kissing you," she snaps back. "That's not the problem."

"Well, the way I see it, you're my best friend, and we like kissing each other. We might as well keep being best friends but add kissing."

She lets go of my tie abruptly, and I have to catch myself on the table with one hand.

"I'm not having this discussion right now."

She's treating me like a child who needs a time-out. Which, granted, I might have earned after making us the center of attention.

But I don't care. I'm going to show her that I'm here for keeps.

Chapter 40

Hazel

Despite me telling Tripp I wasn't scared...I definitely am.

My dad's words echo around my head.

Even Adam said I was scared to participate...

When did I become the person who sheltered down and was scared to put herself out there?

Where has the Hazel gone that was always up for anything—at least once?

Why has it taken me so long to even be willing to entertain out-of-state job offers?

Last night, I emailed *World Mechanic* back about the internship they offered me, and I say yes, depending on the details. Madge immediately sent over a file with more detailed information. I can't believe I'm actually considering leaving.

I slam open the main door to the shop. Maybe I have a piece of metal that needs to be straightened out with a hammer. Maybe I can pound away my frustration.

Tripp hasn't texted or called all week. All I know is he's lost his ever-loving mind. He cannot possibly think that this will work. He's destined to stay here, especially since he's buying that house. I'm dreaming of trying something new— for who knows how long.

I know eventually, I'll be back to Harvest Hollow...but I need to stop playing it safe and spread my wings. I will not live life scared.

I am strong, and I can take the risk.

My personal pep talk is interrupted when my phone rings. I pull it out quickly, but I don't see Tripp's name splashed across the front like I hoped.

It's a spam call.

I groan, shove it back in my pocket, and focus on the car waiting for me.

Milo towed it in yesterday for the owner. It's the same car that had been in recently for a maintenance issue and they didn't bother to have me replace the battery that was struggling.

I pop open the hood and make quick work of the battery leads. How hard would it be for Tripp to text me and tell me if he's still planning on having the auction date tonight?

I grab the battery handle and lift up, feeling my triceps engage.

"If he truly cared, he'd be here," I tell the inanimate object.

Lifting the battery over the edge of the grill, it bangs against the front of my legs.

My legs immediately feel cold...

I drop the battery to the ground and immediately strip

out of my pants. This is what I get for not bothering to put on my coveralls.

A cracked battery spilling acid onto my jeans—my life is charmed. What can I say?

I walk over to the deep sink in the corner, pull off my socks and climb in to rinse.

Splashing cold water on my legs reminds me of Tripp laying cooling cloths on my forehead while I was sick. The way he cared for me—that's the kind of action that makes a person fall in love.

Once I'm satisfied that every hint of battery acid is gone, I climb out of the sink and dry off with the hand towel.

I grab my burning pants and carry them outside to throw them in the trash. There's no salvaging those.

When I turn around, I find Milo standing there looking at me with shock in his eyes. He points to my pantslessness.

"Don't ask," I say as I storm up the steps and into my apartment.

So much for my mantra about not being scared: I shouldn't have left my apartment today. What makes me think I can make it with a big company or in a relationship with Tripp?

I'm not sure how long I lay on my couch, wallowing in despair and telling my irritated, but luckily not-burnt legs that it's okay to have a bad day.

But when there's a loud banging on the door, I realize my wallowing time has run out.

"Hazel. I know you're home. Your dad said you haven't left all day."

"This is a recorded message!" I yell back.

"You've got great voice inflection. Now open up, Miss Answering Machine. I have a message for you."

Knowing Tripp like I do, I'm sure he won't leave until he gets what he wants. So, I slowly trudge to the door and press my forehead to it.

"It's okay, Tripp. I won't hold you to the date we're supposed to have. You were so generous and wonderful, I think we can call it even." My nose hurts from pressing it against the hardwood.

"Are you going back on a promise, Hazelnut?"

It's hard to tell if he's teasing or not when I can't see his face.

I slowly unlatch the door and pull it open.

"Why are your legs so red?" Tripp asks, forgetting all about the date. And I have the uncomfortable realization that I'm standing in front of him—pantsless. Embarrassed. There is no way he could want to be with a wreck like me.

I glance down at said bare legs peeking out beneath my giant sweater. "Oh, I wondered what would happen if I spilled acid on them from a cracked battery."

"You didn't." He sighs as though he's told me five hundred times to stop spilling battery acid on myself.

"I pretty much did. Would you like to see the pants?"

"Yeah, I've always wondered what battery acid does."

"Well, you can't. My pants disintegrated. There's hardly anything left."

"Okay, well, I hope you rinsed your legs for a long time. If you don't, it could still be burning your skin."

I glare at him. "Of course, why didn't I think about that?"

He grins at me knowingly. "Probably because your legs were on fire."

I throw my hands up in exasperation. "It wasn't that bad. I pulled the pants off before it could burn me."

Tripp raises one eyebrow at me. "You were slow answering the door. You must be hurt."

"I think I'm going to set up an alarm bell at the end of the drive. That way I know when you're coming. You're getting this nasty habit of showing up when I embarrass myself or am mad at you."

He clicks his tongue at me. "Now, now. None of that. It's not my fault I keep showing up when something happens to you."

I try my best not to lose my temper. I *really* do. But there's only so much a woman can take.

Chapter 41

Tripp

I realize the second I'm making things worse. And it's when Hazel pivots on me with an icy glare.

Her legs aren't the only thing getting burned today. She's going to leave a few smoldering bodies in her wake—mine being the first.

"Don't look at me like that."

She advances on me. "I'm mad at you.

"Why are you mad at me?" I ask, holding my hands up. "I was just trying to help!"

"I know, Tripp. That's why I'm mad! No matter what you do, it's always for someone else. You're always the good guy. You're always the friend who has done something with his life. You're out there saving lives and I'm still here, Tripp's best friend. I'm just that girl who lives with her dad and changes tires!"

"You know I don't think that!"

"I know, Tripp, that's because you're perfect! And I can never be enough to match that!" Her voice is creeping closer

239

to a yelling level, and I still don't know what we're fighting about. "You got to leave and see the world and go on dates and have an entire life. While I've been here. And then you had to ruin everything by kissing me."

"Is this about me leaving?" Now I feel like yelling because I'd like her to get to the point. "What are we arguing about?"

"You left. And I'm still here. And now you're back wanting to act like everything is fine and that we could just jump into a relationship together. Newsflash: it's not fine! I'm not fine!" she yells.

"I see that!" I grind out. "But you chose to be here! I thought you wanted to be here!"

"I'm not here because I want to be!" she shouts. A chunk of hair falls from the messy bun, falling into her face.

Her eyes are glassy, and she clenches her jaw.

She seems to realize what she just shouted at me. And I can see it all. The hidden pain. Somewhere under this facade of someone who's happily never left home is the little girl who dreamed of going to Ireland. Of visiting Niagara Falls. Of lying on a beach in the Caribbean. And she's stayed. Annie Perkins and my mom...they both saw what I didn't with my best friend.

"I'm sorry. Hazel. I'm so sorry." I say it softly. Knowing that the words mean nothing.

She was here. Holding it together for her sister and her dad. Pretending to fit in a square box. All while she's falling apart inside, and her spirit is being crushed.

I open my arms and take a step toward her. I stand there until the anger fades completely from her eyes, and she steps forward to crumple in my arms.

"I didn't want to stay," her tone is pitiful as she mumbles against my shirt. "Every year, it's getting harder. And what's worse is it's my own fear holding me back now."

Now is not the time to give advice. Right now, I get to hold her, remind her she's special, and tell her it's okay to hurt.

So, I lift her off her feet, carry her inside, and kick the door closed.

"Let's get something straight."

She looks up at me with big blue eyes.

"We're going to find out exactly what you want. From where to live and who you want to be with. But if you can look me in the eye and tell me you've never imagined a future together, I'll walk out that door and pretend like you're just my best friend again. Even though I will never, ever be over you."

She bites her lip.

"So can you honestly tell me that you've never imagined a future with me?"

Chapter 42

Hazel

Tripp's not fighting fair. I'm a horrible liar, and he can always tell. And it's even harder to summon up a lie when I'm hanging on to the front of his shirt.

I have no option but to give him the truth as he's holding me against his chest and my feet aren't even touching the ground.

"Just because I want something doesn't mean I can have it."

Tripp's eyes narrow on me. "And what does that mean?"

I swallow the lump in my throat and whisper, "I might imagine a future with you, but there's too much in the way of letting it happen."

His chest rises and falls slowly as he takes two deep breaths and slowly lowers me to the floor.

"I was scared you didn't care that much for me," he says in a soft voice. A large hand threads through my loose hair before he takes a step back, grabbing me by my shoulders and looking me in the eye. "When have obstacles ever stopped us?"

"But we can't do long distance. I need to go out and try some things. See some places. It's way past time."

"I know, baby."

"I can't make you change the trajectory of your life for me. And I can't give up mine for you. We would eventually resent each other."

He lays his hands against my face, moving closer to me. "No. No, we won't. We can make this work."

"You don't understand! I'm deciding between a job offer at a shop in Colorado and one in Oregon! I want to travel, and you're staying here!"

His hands press against my cheeks. "But I'm not staying without you!"

It's hard to get your words out when someone is squishing your cheeks. Squished cheek words just aren't the same.

"Bish avu aby ay."

He releases my cheeks, and his thumbs gently brush away those sneaky tears.

"But you moved home to stay," I state, as though I know his mind better than him...which I'm beginning to think I don't.

He tilts my face up to look at him. "You are the reason I'm here."

"But your job is here."

He shakes his head once. "My contract at the hospital is for six months. I'm already through two months of it. After those six months, I can look for anything."

He's smiling softly at me as though he would give up his dreams for me. That would shatter my heart as well.

"But you love Harvest Hollow."

"Yes, Hazel. But I need you to listen to me. I've lived in Arizona and Oregon and loved those places. But they were missing something. I came back to Harvest Hollow. But it still felt like it was missing something. Until you. Until I saw you by that in that grocery store looking so adorable in your sweatpants. That was when I felt like I had come home. Whether you want to live here or somewhere halfway around the world, I'm with you."

My chest feels like it's cracking at his words. "You've got to stop. I have fake lashes on, and I swear if you make me cry, it's going to melt the glue," I sob.

"I realized that what was missing in every place I've been...is you."

I lean forward and plant my forehead against his chest.

"Harvest Hollow will always be special to me. But my home is with you. Do you know how hard I tried to find someone to replace you? I couldn't find anyone because there's only one Hazel Preston in this world."

"You're taking the words right out of my mouth," I mumble against his now-wet long-sleeve shirt.

"I love you, Hazel. I've always loved you. It's always been you. You've been number one in my life. I don't ever want that to change."

I grab fistfuls of his shirt as if that will hold him tight to me. His arms are strong around me, and I hope he never, ever lets me go. We'll have to learn how to walk like this.

I finally tell him the truth. "It wrecked me, thinking

about us not being together. I didn't want to let you go, but it wasn't fair of me to ask you to change your dream."

"Hazel, you are my dream. Making a life together? That's my dream. Don't get me wrong, I love being a doctor. But I can do that anywhere. Turns out there are people all across this country getting sick or doing dumb things and ending up in the ER."

"Tripp, I *want* to be with you. Because...I love you too. If we're going to make this work, I don't expect you always to be the one giving something up." I clear my throat. "Unless it's chocolate. I always expect you to share that."

"I would never expect you to give up chocolate for me. But you are going to have to share the pumpkin bread."

I raise my arms to wrap them around his neck. "What if we mess up?"

"We probably will," he replies as he wraps his arms around my waist.

"That's not exactly a vote of confidence." I frown at him.

"People mess up, Hazel. But guess what? I love you even when you mess up. And I know you feel the same. We'll work through it, whatever it is."

"How can you be so confident?"

"Because you're my soulmate." He bends down and kisses me before I can reply. Or break out in happy tears.

Mr. Find His Soulmate just confessed that I'm it.

He's not settling for someone who's a placeholder. I'm his match. And he's mine.

I only wish it hadn't taken us this long to figure out the obvious.

Moaning, I grasp his shirt collar and pull him closer to deepen the kiss. My chest aches in the best possible way.

Tripp loves me.

"Get in." He points to his car at the bottom of my stairs. The door is wide open again and the cold air is rushing in.

I thought we should finish the date in my apartment. Tripp told me he wasn't going to start out dating me lazily. That he was going to take me to dinner, and we were getting champagne to celebrate.

I look down at my oversized sweater and bare legs.

"But I'm not wearing pants." Goose bumps appear on my legs as that cold fall air blows inside.

"That's okay. You look great." His eyes sweep up and down once before he motions to the car.

I fold my arms over my chest. "I'm not leaving without pants."

He holds his arm out to stare at his smartwatch. "Thirty seconds then, I'm throwing you in the car, pants or no pants."

"Thirty seconds is not enough time to—"

He cuts me off, "I'm already counting."

"Tripp," I start to complain, but then his smile takes on an evil glint, and I know he's not joking. I spin around and run to my bedroom. I frantically search through the mountain of clothes on my bed, find some jeans and run back to the front of the apartment, trying to pull them on without falling on my face.

"Time's up!"

My heart skips a beat as Tripp appears in the doorway. That smile is downright sinister now. "Oops."

I only have one leg in the pants, and I can't catch my breath between my laughter as he bends down and lifts me over his shoulder, pants dangling from one ankle.

Thank goodness for oversized sweaters and granny panties.

"If you drop me on my head…"

"Maybe it will balance out that time you decided to jump the dirt bike on the high school track."

"Right." The blood is rushing to my head, but it doesn't block out the memory of what was one of the funniest events in high school.

Someone had left some plywood lying on the high school track. What was I supposed to do with it?

Jump it, of course.

Needless to say, my motorcycle days were short-lived.

"Tripp, where are we going to dinner?"

"Somewhere delicious to celebrate."

"Hmm, feeling proud of yourself, are you?" I ask as I rest a hand on his lower back, pressing myself upward as he reaches the car.

"Tripp, I know a lot of places have a no shoes, no shirt, no service policy. What's everyone's take on no pants?" His only answer is to throw back his head and laugh before he sets me in the front seat of his car.

Life with him will never be dull.

Chapter 43

Hazel

Delucca's Italian restaurant is packed. Luckily, since it's only the two of us, we don't have to wait long.

We sit down with a nice red wine and enough breadsticks to feed a small army. To top it all off, we're holding hands in public.

I feel guilty.

It's like someone is going to point at us and yell "faker" at any minute. But that still doesn't discourage me from holding Tripp's hand. My fingers are laced through his, and we don't let go, no matter what.

"See? I told you somewhere yummy to celebrate," he teases as he dips a breadstick in alfredo sauce.

"You were right," I say as I struggle to break a breadstick in half with one hand. Tripp reaches over to help me out.

"We've successfully eaten a whole basket of breadsticks together. I'm pretty sure there's nothing we can't conquer as a couple," Tripp says with a smile.

"Shhh, it still sounds weird. And it's only been five minutes, I'm not sure you can call us a couple," I tease him.

He leans forward and narrows his eyes at me. "From now on, Hazelnut, I'm calling it like it is."

I blush but don't break his gaze.

"I love you, Hazel. I don't need to date you to find out what I already know. I'm sticking with you."

"Shh, you can't make me cry in public."

He looks at me a moment longer before he takes pity on my fragile emotional state and leans back in his chair. "Speaking of shushing, you still haven't told me about this internship."

Blowing a slow breath between my lips, I lean forward and rest an elbow on the table. It's the moment where both my dreams collide. So I spend the next twenty minutes explaining the details of the internship at the World Mechanic shop and how I'd be able to finish out my L3 certification there.

"You sound really excited about this, Hazel. When is it?"

"The next training round starts next month," I say quietly.

"And where is this training?"

"Denver," I whisper.

Tripp's eyes brighten. "You've always wanted to go to Colorado. If you take this, we'll be able to do all sorts of snowboarding."

"If we weren't in a busy restaurant right now, I would kiss you," I declare.

Tripp looks around slowly. "Don't let that stop you."

"You're really supportive of this?"

He sighs. "Hazel. I know you think that somehow, some

way I'm going to magically forget who you are, or what your dreams are. But I'm here to stay. And I'm going to keep showing up for you and keep supporting you in whatever area you need it."

I lean forward and plant a quick kiss on his lips, bumping a wine glass and nearly knocking it over.

It's worth the shocked gasp from the table next to us.

Chapter 44

Tripp

"Why are we sitting in a town council meeting?" I whisper to Hazel. It's been a week since our first date as a couple. I didn't know a person could almost die from being happy, but I've come close.

She looks at me with a slight frown. "Because we're concerned citizens of Harvest Hollow who want to bring up the parking issue."

Ha. This is probably the beginning of a good fight in front of the entire town. I'd like to see Hazel take on Wayne Oakley. She might actually take him down a peg or two.

I hold my hand out flat and she immediately places her hand in it, lacing her fingers through mine.

This will never get old. It's been an entire week of dating, and it's started to be physically painful to be apart. I'm already buying plane tickets to visit her when she's in Denver for nine weeks. It's so strange to be excited for someone but sad at the thought of them leaving.

"I'd like to make mention of the giant pumpkin on the

sidewalk in front of City Hall." The mayor shakes his head as he looks around the room. I haven't heard a word of the other things he said, and if he's going to waste time talking about a pumpkin, then I'm happy I tuned him out. "While we appreciate the fall spirit, especially since it's our kind of thing, the amount of people taking pictures with it is clogging up traffic. Wayne Oakley kindly left a note on it stating it was his contribution to this wonderful fall town. Unfortunately, he's not here today so that he can take it back to his house. Does anyone know when he'll be back?"

No one raises their hand.

"I'll have no choice but to hire Biff's towing with city funds to remove it and put it back on his property, then. He has a lovely home that will make the perfect backdrop for all the pumpkin pictures."

Still, no one moves a muscle besides lots of chuckles.

I turn to look at Hazel. No laughter there...just a small little twitch at the corner of her mouth.

I lean over and whisper in her ear, "How did you get the pumpkin to City Hall?"

She turns to look at me with shocked, wide eyes. "What on earth are you talking about?"

I narrow my eyes at her. "You know."

She shakes her head, but those lips are still twitching. "Tripp Sharpe. I can't believe you would accuse me of something so immature."

She turns back to listen to the mayor. That lip twitch is starting to turn into a full smile.

Yup, that definitely was her. And she somehow did it in the name of Wayne Oakley.

"I can't believe you didn't tell me you were going to do that," I whisper to her.

She leans over and whispers, "I didn't want you to stoop to my level."

"I'll happily stoop to your level anytime." I lean over and press a quick kiss against her cheek.

She turns and looks up at me with those big blue eyes. "I love you, Dr. Tripp Sharpe. And I can't think of anyone I would rather get into mischief with."

"I love you, Hazel. And I can't imagine anyone I would rather keep out of mischief."

She grins at me as she says, "You realize it's a lifetime job, right?"

"I wouldn't have it any other way. Soulmates are forever, you know."

This time when I lean over to kiss her, it's not slow.

And it's the first time I've been kicked out of a meeting for Public Displays of Affection.

Epilogue

Hazel

T ripp is waiting for me when I get off the airplane. He's standing as close to the arrivals gate as he can get.

The TSA officer guarding the exit looks nervous at his close proximity. As though Tripp might dart through and leap on a plane heading for Hawaii.

I'm just getting back from my internship with the *World's Mechanic* office. I now have my L3 certification and have some more hands-on experience than I could have ever gotten on my own.

I hurry forward and swing my bag more onto my back so that I can jump into his arms.

He catches me without hesitation and bends down to kiss me. I never knew that Tripp would be so physically affectionate. But anytime we're together, he's touching me.

What's funny—is I feel the same way. I can't get enough of him.

When we finally pull apart, I have an embarrassing urge to happy cry.

Tripp rubs a thumb gently across my cheek. "Want to move to a different state?"

Three weeks into the training, I called Tripp and told him I wanted to come home—home to him, and home to Harvest Hollow. Traveling will always be fun, but I know exactly where I belong now.

I shake my head. "I want to go home."

And that's just what we do. We load up in Tripp's car (he ignores my offer to drive) and start our way to Harvest Hollow from Knoxville.

"Before I drop you off at home, I want to show you something."

"Keep them closed." Tripp holds my hand and pulls me out of the car.

The stinker blindfolded me when we pulled into Harvest Hollow.

He keeps telling me that it will be worth the wait. And it's making me question how well he knows me. Because I *hate* waiting.

"Just trust me," he says. His fingers lace through mine, and I take some stumbling steps after him. I'm walking on concrete.

So, I can only assume it's a sidewalk of some sort.

"OK, open your eyes." Trip yanks the covering—a pair of my own sweatpants from my bag—off my eyes, and I look around to get my bearings. I'm not standing on the sidewalk. I'm standing in a building. A large building.

The car is parked inside and there's a large, closed rolling door.

There's a chain hoist and a set of ramps. A car lift is in the center and the walls are lined with shelves and pegboard. There's a welding set in the corner. Heck, that's my welding set.

"What is this?"

Tripp drops down onto one knee, my eyes widen as I stare at him.

"What the heck are you doing?"

"Hush, you're ruining my romantic moment." He pulls out a box and flips it open to reveal a ring. The most gorgeous ring I've ever seen. The three diamonds are set in the band, making the ring relatively flat. It looks like something Tripp would have designed himself. It looks like a beautiful ring that a mechanic could wear under gloves.

It's the second time I've had to fight back tears in one day. Tripp's trying to set records.

"Hazel Preston, would you do the honor of becoming my wife?"

I stare at him. We've been dating now for three months. Nine of those weeks I've been gone. Granted, somehow the guy managed to fly over Denver every other week and we talked every single day on the phone.

Is this fast? I don't know.

Is it right? 100%. There's no question in my mind. There are zero doubts. I know exactly what I'm getting into if I marry Tripp.

If I say yes, it'll be the best decision I've ever made in my life.

"I'll say yes, only if you think you'll be happy being stuck with me."

He grins up at me. "I would say it'd be 'easy as pie' but we both know we'll have our fights."

"Why are you proposing to me in a shop?"

"Because it's my engagement present to you if you'll say yes."

"So, you're bribing me to say yes?" I fold my arms across my chest and do my best to scowl at him.

"I'm willing to do whatever necessary to tip the scale in my favor." He smiles softly at me.

I kneel down in front of him and wrap my arms around his neck. "You don't have to do anything to convince me. All you have to do is be yourself and I'd gladly spend the rest of my life with you."

"Same for me, Hazelnut," Tripp whispers in my ear before he pulls back to press a kiss against my lips. "You're sure you want to spend your life here with me? I'll go anywhere where you are."

The serious look in his eyes shows me that he means it.

"I think I've fallen in love with the idea of going on trips and coming home to Harvest Hollow. What about you?" I shift uncomfortably because concrete is hard and cold, and I don't know how Tripp has been kneeling down here so long.

"*You* are home, Hazel. Wherever you are is home to me."

I grin at him. "Then you better put a ring on it and make it official."

Sweater Weather

Thank you for reading into Easy as Pie! If you want to read more in the adorable town of Harvest Hollow, check out the rest of the series here!

Sweater Weather Series

BONUS SCENE

Not ready to say goodbye to Tripp and Hazel? I'm not either!

You can find a fun bonus scene HERE!

Read about their first trip together when you sign up for my newsletter!

Also by Carina Taylor

Forget Me Twice (Archie and Meyer's story)

Have you ever brought your ex-husband home and pretended to still be married? Yeah, me either.

When my local hospital calls to say "I'm sorry to tell you this, but your husband has been in an accident" I try to explain the basics to them.

1 I am not married—anymore. (Archie Dunmore is a thing of the past.)

2 If there's a husband in the hospital, it's not mine.

Except Archie is back, and he's been in an accident. One that has left him with amnesia. Yup. He believes we're still happily married. *Oh joy.*

Too bad for me, the doctor believes it would be best for Archie to remember things on his own. He needs familiar surroundings to heal.

No big shocks. No emotional trauma.

Which means I can't tell him the truth.

Archie bursts back into my life with all the warmth and joy of a freshly married man, confident that I'm the love of his life, and determined to fix the rift between us.

Except how do I tell him that he walked out on me?

Especially when Archie is desperately trying to remember what I've worked so hard to forget.

What's a girl to do with an amnesiac ex-husband at her breakfast table?

Play Me Once (Willa and Kingston's story)

Kingston Palmer is **public enemy number one.**

Pain in the butt.

Bane of my existence.

An overgrown nuisance that looks good in a suit.

To Kingston, I'm nothing more than a game. One that he's sure he can win.

Don't worry; he underestimates my *own* dedication to winning.

Unfortunately for me, I accidentally signed on to work at his company (yes, yes, it's a loooong story).

Kingston is my new boss.

But I'm nothing if not efficient. I'll be an expert at my job all while dutifully ignoring my boss and his ability to lean on door frames.

My task is to create a nonprofit that benefits the community. Easy peasy.

It's everything else that gets complicated: avoiding my boss, making the required snide comments, and turning him down for dates is turning into a full-time job all on its own.

It's not like he *actually* wants me. *At least, I don't think so...*

Acknowledgments

TO ALL MY READERS. It's scary putting your words out in the world—scary creating a story and an entire world then releasing it for public consumption. But you all make it worth it, every single time. Thank you for loving these stories! Thank you for your support and love for these characters! Every review, every message, booktok, bookstagram post, they all mean so much to me. Thank you for everything!

Gigi, Rachel, Aspen, Sophie. Thanks for being so amazing and walking through this whole authoring thing with me. Gigi and Rachel you made this story so much stronger! I couldn't do this without you ladies! (And also can't wait for all our brilliant genre mashups we've dreamed up. ;))

Kirsten, Courtney, Melanie, Julie, Patty, Jenny... I had so much fun working on this series with all of you. You made writing such a fun group effort! You're all wonderful, and hopefully, we have our Ethans under control in the future.

Thank you to all of my ARC readers! Thank you for being the first readers to take a chance on this story. I loved getting to talk with you all about your favorite parts. Thank you for falling in love with Tripp and Hazel! (And thanks for loving chapter 33.)

Made in the USA
Middletown, DE
27 September 2024

61576704R00163